Mickey twisted the ignition key and the T-Bird responded. He drove along the driveway and was heading for the street. Sonya, sitting beside Mickey with an inward readiness for the unexpected, saw it first.

A dark green station wagon screeched to a halt and blocked the driveway. It appeared quite suddenly, as though out of nowhere. A side door of the station wagon flew open. A bushy-haired youth balanced a double-barreled shotgun.

Even though she was amazed that anyone was aware of the money, Sonya assumed that it was a heist. She moved just in time. A loud, fiery explosion flew from the mouth of the shotgun. Sonya, however, had opened the car door and rolled onto the driveway. The windshield of the T-Bird instantly disappeared, as did Mickey's entire head.

Another bushy-haired youth leaped from the front of the station wagon and threw a Molotov cocktail. It traveled through the jagged hole where the windshield had once been. The T-Bird was immediately engulfed in flames.

The money! The money! Sonya could not allow them to take the money. It represented all she had ever planned for, schemed for, and quite frequently gone along with murder for. She stood quite straight as she ran toward her attackers, the automatic weapon belching forth death!
  —*THE BLACK CONNECTION*

Other Holloway House Original editions
by Randolph Harris:

THE TERRORISTS

TRICKSHOT

THE LIFE AND TIMES OF JONATHAN GOODE

als/30

THE BLACK CONNECTION

by RANDOLPH HARRIS

AN ORIGINAL HOLLOWAY HOUSE EDITION

HOLLOWAY HOUSE PUBLISHING CO.
LOS ANGELES, CALIFORNIA

Published by
HOLLOWAY HOUSE PUBLISHING COMPANY
8060 Melrose Avenue, Los Angeles, CA 90046
All rights reserved. No part of this book may be reproduced or transmitted in any form or by any means, electronic or mechanical, including photocopying, recording or by any information storage and retrieval system, without permission in writing from the Publisher.
Copyright © 1974, 1987 by Randolph Harris.
Any similarity to persons living or dead is purely coincidental.
International Standard Book Number 0-87067-271-1
Printed in the United States of America
Cover design by Claudia Warner

DEDICATED TO

the fellows at Julia's Place.

R.H.

chapter 1

IT ALL BEGAN on Chicago's south side. The public records will reveal that it was far from a tranquil city.

Charles Dumont was a product of Chicago's south side ghetto. Recently released from the state penitentiary, Dumont had completed a two year prison term for the sale of narcotics and had been free for only three weeks.

Charles Dumont entered the drug store at 47th Street and St. Lawrence Avenue. He headed into the phone booth, picked up the receiver and dropped a dime. A man's voice answered.

"Hello, Monk? . . . Charlie."

THE BLACK CONNECTION

"Hi, Charlie, meet me at the bar."

"Will do."

Dumont, a short, dark-skinned man about twenty-five years old, replaced the receiver and sauntered out of the busy drug store.

The night was hot and sultry. The vendor was blasting at the 808 Club, which was only two doors from the drug store. The sweet shop across the street was highly active, as were the multitude of shops up and down 47th Street.

There were a couple of taverns to every block as far as the eye could see. Barbecue houses, supermarkets, restaurants, liquor stores, tailor shops, neighborhood grocery stores: all were doing very effective business. Cabs were honking at impatient jaywalkers and the behind schedule buses would also join the tirade. Music could be heard coming from the dwellings above the hot and crowded streets.

Furtive figures using street corner telephone booths, clandestine persons hovering in doorways, all presented a rather perplexing scene. To a few, perhaps, the scene appeared quite puzzling. But to others, who were more aware, it was within the ordinary.

One could stroll by the mouth of an alley and see an individual pitifully puking up his guts, or one might enter a bar and see a few local residents

by Randolph Harris

taking drugful siestas.

To the two Federal agents who had just cruised past the cab stand near the corner of Vincennes Avenue, these were not uncommon scenes. This populous community of perplexity was vastly and most rapidly becoming "Dopeville, U.S.A." At least, in the eyes of the city's daily papers which had, of course, issued that statement.

There was a wooden door, badly in need of paint, stuck between the cleaners and the 808 Club. This door led to a long ascending stairway, and eventually to a few kitchenette apartments above.

Charles Dumont entered this door and mounted the creaking stairs. The time was 10:05 P.M., when Dumont greeted seven other occupants who already were in the dingy abode.

Mickey, a short, dark-skinned lad with processed hair, was the first to greet Dumont. "Hi, ole dude, glad to see you home." The remaining persons in the shabby apartment took turns in their handshaking receptions.

Four of the young men, whose ages ranged from 22 to 26 years, were sitting around an old dining room table. You know the kind: round, wooden, and it expanded so an extra panel could be interjected to make it larger.

One of the three youths who were spaced along

THE BLACK CONNECTION

the green faded couch spoke up. "Where is the Monk? He said that he would be here at ten o'clock."

"Oh, he'll be along any minute," Charles Dumont answered. "I just talked to him. That's why I'm here."

Another young man of dark complexion came out of the toilet and settled in an old upholstered lounge chair which had seen its best days. A knock was heard at the door. One of the young men lifted himself from the couch and opened the door.

Monk stood in the doorway. Tall—6'2" to be exact—black-skinned and strong-boned, he must have weighed at least 225 pounds. Oscar (Monk) Davis was twenty-nine years old, and his features were as thick as his speech.

"All of you fellas know Charlie?"

"Yeah, man." Red, one man from the couch, spoke up. "He and I went to school together. Right, dude?"

"Right," Charles answered, turning to look at Red.

There were other nods and comments from the remaining persons. All were positive.

Monk was standing by the much scarred dresser. Its mirror had a small crack along the top corner and a couple of drawers were handleless. This rundown apartment was used as a sort of clubroom.

by Randolph Harris

Monk had had one of his girl friends rent it under a bogus name five years ago and since then it had never been decorated. But it was conveniently located over the tavern in which most of the fellows present hung out. In fact, the tavern downstairs was their headquarters.

Monk continued, "I told Charlie to meet me here because, as you all know, he had just started with us when he took his fall." Monk leaned back on the dilapidated dresser, then turned his head toward Charlie. "Things have changed quite a bit since you have been gone."

There were nods of confirmation; otherwise, everyone remained silent and attentive. Monk went on. "If things had been run the way they are now, you would have never had to do that bit." Monk bowed his head to Charlie. "You see, Charlie, now we play for keeps just like the white boys do. We don't take oaths and things like that, but we let it be known that we don't tolerate no shit."

Monk reached to his shirt pocket and brought out a package of cigarettes. He produced a lighter from his sport coat pocket and the flame flared; then he continued. "If we had taken care of that little punk who took the stand against you, you would have never had to do a day. Since you've been gone, however, there have been a couple of incidents, but we beat the cases because we had the

THE BLACK CONNECTION

sources removed."

Charlie Dumont, who was sitting in a straight back wooden chair, interrupted. "Say, man, what happened to Johnny? You know, the dude who flipped on me?"

Monk listened attentively, then answered. "Aw, he's supposed to be somewhere down south—Alabama, I think it is. He left right after the case was over. Don't worry, he'll never come back this way. It would have done no good to off him after you had gotten your time. The damage had already been done. But now things are different, which you will soon learn. If we find out about a pigeon in time, you can bet he'll never take the stand against any of us."

Around the dingy apartment agreeable comments could be heard. "And I think," Monk went on, "that the last dude they found has let the brothers across the country know that." Again murmurs were heard in accord.

Charlie Dumont duffed his cigarette and interrupted again. "But how do we find out about the pigeons? You know how they protect so many of them. Why, when I was in County jail waiting to be shipped, I found out about a whole tier that housed nothing but stool-pigeons. They ate and slept there. They let them out, or even sometimes took them out when there were things they wanted

by Randolph Harris

them to do: such as set up some dealer."

"Oh, we have our own ways of finding out," Monk said. "You see, Charlie, everybody likes money. That is to say, the police. Now when it comes to the government, that's where we have to be extra careful; those agents don't go for no shit."

At approximately 11:15 P.M., Charles Dumont was seen coming out of the wooden door entrance. Parked at the corner of 47th and Vincennes Avenue was a dark brown car which contained two white men, Agents Daniel Gruff and Sidney Miller, who had had the tavern and its patrons under surveillance for the last two months.

Agent Gruff, well groomed and soft spoken, did not give the appearance of a custodian. He had a thin crop of mixed grey hair, amiable features and an amazing understanding and compassion for the downtrodden and misguided. However, he bore a deadly unforgiveness for the peddlers of destruction. He had been with the Federal Bureau of Narcotics for nine years and was an avowed stickler of the law.

Agent Sidney E. Miller, an eight-year veteran of the Federal Narcotics Bureau, was a man whose ruggedly pock-marked face portrayed the sternness of his character. He sat beside Agent Gruff. The two agents watched Charles Dumont as he stepped

THE BLACK CONNECTION

from the wooden door and entered the 808 Club.

"Well," Gruff said, "it looks like the meeting is over."

Agent Miller's face waxed as he answered. "Yeah, but where is the 'Monk'?"

"Aw, he'll be down shortly. Probably briefing some of the guys on their next move."

Leaning toward the windshield, Agent Miller said, "Who is that, Dan?"

"That one is called 'Beany'. He's been with the outfit ever since they called themselves an 'organization,'" Gruff answered.

"Oh, yeah," said Miller. "He's the guy we followed from the Monk's house that night. He looks a little different from here."

Agent Gruff's face revealed a smile. "Yeah, he's had his hair processed. Here comes two more." Now Gruff was squinting beyond the windshield.

"Yeah," answered Miller, "and one of them looks like the Monk. He's got on that suede outfit. He really likes to dress casual."

Gruff slid down in his seat and pulled his hat over his eyes. "Well," he said, "if they run true to form we'll be here until closing time. In the meantime, keep your eyes open." Saying that, Agent Gruff folded his arms and leaned back in his seat.

"You bet," answered Miller, and began his lonely vigil.

by Randolph Harris

Inside the bar, Monk was gingerly pawing the body of a petite, light-complexioned girl who was responding with giggles.

"Dolly," Monk said, gesturing toward Dumont, "this is Charlie—Charlie Dumont."

"Hi," Dumont nodded.

"Hello, Charlie," Dolly said, still giggling. "Glad to know you."

Dolly spun around on the bar stool and peered up at Monk. "Gonna take me with you when you leave?"

"I don't know," Monk answered. "I've got to make a call first."

The men who had been upstairs had entered the bar. Slick, the bartender, was now quite busy pouring drinks.

The 808 Club was nothing to write home and tell the folks about. Just the usual groupings of colored lights, medium length bar and eight or ten wooden stools. There were two square-topped tables in the middle of the floor and two wooden booths to the left. That was about it. But the regulars liked it and felt comfortable there.

Charlie Dumont noticed that Monk was dialing the wall telephone after dropping an unusual amount of coins. Shortly Monk hung up and sauntered over to Dolly. "Naw, baby, I don't think we can goof off tonight. I've got things to do."

THE BLACK CONNECTION

Disappointed, Dolly responded, "Aw, and I had some swell things planned for both of us."

Long, slim fingers were crawling up the front of Monk's chest. "Yeah, I know, but they'll have to wait till later," Monk said, pushing her hands down and turning toward Charlie Dumont.

Handing Dumont a twenty-dollar bill, Monk said, "Here man, pay the bar bill while I say something to Red. Then I want you to go with me."

Monk, a high school graduate who had served time shortly after receiving his diploma, began speaking to Red who, much like the rest of the gathering, was a grade school dropout.

Dumont approached Monk. "You ready?"

"Yeah," Monk turned to Red. "I'll dig you later, dude."

Back at the agent's car, Miller touched his snoozing partner's arm. "Looks as though they've broken the pattern tonight."

Agent Gruff was alerted, pushing his hat straight.

He arched his body and peered. "Yep, that's the Monk, all right, and he's got the new recruit with him."

"It looks like we're going for a ride," Miller said, as he reached for the ignition key.

"Yeah," Gruff answered, "but be careful. This

by Randolph Harris

damn street is busier than those in Tokyo."

"They're getting in Monk's car, all right. Say, this bunch of guys differ from the rest. They don't go in for the big Cadillac cars like most of the dealers do."

"Yeah," Gruff answered. "The chief briefed us on that, remember? It appears that this guy Monk varies from the average ghetto pattern altogether. He dresses rather conservatively. He doesn't wear flashy jewelry. He doesn't gamble; that is, until he sneaks off to Vegas. He doesn't frequent the bars or the after-hour joints; and damn it, most of his outfit follows his policy. It makes it rather difficult for our informants to stay alerted to their activities."

"Well," Miller said, "his M.O. shows that he runs a tight and well-organized outfit. In fact, those two killings last month have scared the pants off the average informer. It's gotten to the point where the informers are shaking their heads as soon as you mention any of Monk's people's names."

"Yeah, the mob's becoming quite a problem, all right. Watch it! Go around that truck. If we get caught by a red light, we'll never spot them in this traffic."

"Yeah," Miller stated. "That Olds won't be easy to pick out in an ordinary group of cars. Looks like he's turning. That's good."

THE BLACK CONNECTION

The two agents followed the dark gray Olds along South Park Boulevard, then up the ramp on 24th Street and toward the Dan Ryan Expressway. Once on the Dan Ryan, it headed due north.

"Where do you think he's going?"

Gruff seemed puzzled. "I don't rightly know. If it was daytime, and knowing his flair for the races, I'd say the racetrack. But . . . I just don't know."

After miles of lane changing and eye-straining maneuvering, the lights of O'Hare Airport appeared in the night sky.

"He's an unpredictable son-of-a-bitch, all right." Miller was guiding his car into the airport lane, which was the same lane the Olds had taken.

"Do you think they're coming to meet someone with a delivery?"

Agent Gruff mashed out his cigarette in the ashtray. "I don't think so," he replied shortly.

Miller looked at Gruff, who had that familiar expression on his face which Agent Miller had seen before.

"All right, Sherlock," Miller said, "when you get it together, enlighten me, will you?"

"It just doesn't figure," Gruff replied. "Remember last year when the Bureau intercepted that package and goofed?"

"Of course. I was on an assignment in Lebanon at the time, but I heard about it."

by Randolph Harris

"Well," Gruff went on, "the package was addressed to the Monk. An agent had followed it all the way from New York City. But somewhere along the line—I don't know if it was the postal authorities or if it was the Bureau—however, the decision was made that the package should be opened to verify its contents."

"Oh! I get it," interrupted Miller. "If it hadn't contained narcotics, the Monk would have been tipped that the Bureau was watching him."

"Exactly!" stated Gruff. "Anyway, just as it had been figured, the package contained a kilo of heroin. However, when the case came to trial, Monk's attorney convinced the jury that by a previous opening anyone could have placed the heroin in the package. Thus, Monk was acquitted."

"Yeah," Miller said. "I think that case set a precedent."

"So, I can't see the Monk using such antique methods as getting his deliveries by plane; he's just too ingenious for that." Gruff was pondering.

"He's going up the 'Arrival' ramp," Miller indicated.

Vibrations from the overhead planes shook the ground as the agents' car approached the ramp. A cab had stopped abruptly to pick up a gesturing pedestrian.

"That prick!" Miller cussed at the cabbie.

THE BLACK CONNECTION

"Monk's parking, anyway," stated Gruff.

"Over there! It looks like that guy's ready to pull out." Agent Gruff was pointing at the potential parking space which was six or seven cars behind the dark gray Oldsmobile.

At that moment, Monk got out of his car, leaving Dumont. He sprinted across the concrete median, and entered the terminal.

The agents were watching him. "You keep an eye on the car," Gruff remarked, "and I'll tail the Monk."

"Check!"

Passengers were crowding in and out of the terminal. Agent Gruff caught a glimpse of the brown suede jacket as Monk mounted the escalator. He followed his man through the packed terminal.

Oscar (Monk) Davis hurried to terminal number five. He stopped once and checked his watch. Luggage carriers saturated the passageway. Loudspeakers were giving out information. Monk stopped at Gate Five as the loudspeaker erupted. "Flight 738 arriving at Gate Five, on time." Monk looked at his diamond dial watch and appreciated that it was also on time.

The plane was emptying as Monk towered above the crowd and scanned. Jostling amongst the deplaning passengers was a medium height man of

by Randolph Harris

dapper dress. The wide fedora hat bounced above his thick black hair and horn-rimmed glasses as he strode with quickened steps. If one was forced to guess his nationality, the suntan may have caused confusion. But when he ambled over to Monk and spoke, there was no doubt that he was Sicilian.

"Oscar, my boy, you looka fine."

"Hi, Bonito," Monk said, as he shook the dark Sicilian's hand. "How was the flight?"

"It awright, I guess. But you know, Oscar, I no like da planes. I get enough of dem durin' da war."

Monk looked at Bonito. "That's right. You were a prisoner during the war, weren't you?"

"Yeah, yeah." The two men shuffled through the terminal as though unaware of the pressing throng of humanity.

Bonito Serritelli, thirty-five years old, had been in the United States two years; a feat accomplished through the efforts of an older naturalized uncle, Santino Serritelli.

Monk had met Bonito a year earlier in a clandestine gathering which was arranged by Uncle Santino.

"How is Santino? I called him tonight to see what time you were arriving."

Bonito hunched his shoulders and waved his hands as he answered, "He okay, Oscar. A little crabby, but he still okay."

"Well, you know how that is, Bonito," Monk remarked, turning to look at his companion as they reached the descending elevator. "He's getting up there. How old is he now?"

"He be . . . ah, sixty-five soon, I think."

"Over this way." Monk was pointing. "I've got this friend with me that I've been telling you about. He's only been home about three weeks."

"He good boy, huh?"

"Now would I introduce him if he wasn't?"

"I sorry, Oscar." Bonito gave Monk a faint pat on the shoulder.

When the dark gray Oldsmobile pulled away from the curb, Charles Dumont was driving. The gray car headed south with its three occupants. By the time the car turned at Lake Street, heading for the downtown Loop, the conversation had taken on an argumentative shade.

"But why?" Monk asked the man sitting next to him, "should the delivery route be changed now? Things seem to be working okay with the boxes coming by train. It's much slower, but it's less suspicious."

"I know," Bonito said, gesturing animatedly with his hands, "but Santino say that if something lost this way, no one held responsible. He no like. He want someone with merchandise all the

by Randolph Harris

time ... I think he right." Bonito shrugged his shoulders and flicked his hands.

"Yeah," Monk said. "But nothing has been lost yet."

"What you do?" asked Bonito. "Wait till something lost before make change?"

"Well, I guess you've got a point there," Monk responded.

Dumont, though it went unobserved, was forced to smile on hearing the rebuttal that had transpired in the rear of the car.

"So the stuff will come through Canada from now on?" Monk asked.

"Dat'sa right," Bonito clarified.

"Damn it, Bonito, I don't understand Santino. Why take a chance with the customs at the border when we don't have to worry about them if we ship by train?"

"My uncle, Santino, very smart man. He say dis is racing season. Thousands of cars leave Windsor Racetrack at night, returning to the city of Detroit. Customs no bother to search. He in this country long time. He *experto credo*."

"Damn it, Bonito, I've told you about that damn talk before. Now what does that mean?"

"Like I say, Oscar," Bonito was gesturing with his hands again, "Santino in this country long time—yet have no trouble. *Experto credo*. It mean:

23

THE BLACK CONNECTION

Trust one who have experience."

Dumont looked in the rear view mirror and interjected, "He's right about that racetrack bit, Monk. I was there once before I went to the joint, and like he says, they can't possibly search all those returning cars when the races are over. Cars pour across that border by the thousands."

"He send me here to tell you," Bonito continued. "You know, he no lika tha telephone."

"Well," Monk said, as he reached for a cigarette, "the old man's been right so far. I guess that's why he runs the show."

"You stick wit him; you be rich man." Bonito turned and looked at Monk as he spoke.

The car pulled up and stopped in front of the Palmer House Hotel on the Wabash Avenue side. Bonito got out and said, "I call your house in hour. Let you know what room, okay?"

"Fine, Bonito." Monk also was on the sidewalk, about to take the front seat next to Dumont.

Charlie Dumont drove the car away and continued south. Monk attempted to say something, but the overhead L-train drowned out his voice. Dumont turned left and then headed south along Michigan Boulevard.

"I hope," Monk said to Dumont, "that Red took care of that business."

"Was it real important?"

by Randolph Harris

"Not exactly. Just a little punk who owes some money. And I don't want him to think I've forgotten about it."

chapter 2

RED, A SLENDER, BONY-FACED MAN, could be seen walking up the well-trodden stairs of a rundown apartment building at 50th Street. He came to the second floor and turned left into the long, dimly lit hallway. He unbuttoned his green checkered sportcoat and readjusted his .38 snubnose revolver. It was merely a precautionary gesture. After all, the man he was about to visit was nothing but a lamb.

Red stopped in front of apartment 208. He could hear the radio giving out with jazz. He knocked two times and heard the radio volume go down; then he heard a lady's timid voice ask, ":Who is it?"

"I want to speak to Bob."

There was a faint sound like the shuffling of feet, then the door was opened. Red stepped into the shabby abode. He was greeted by a small, brown-skinned woman with noticeably large eyes.

THE BLACK CONNECTION

"Have a seat," she said, pointing to the bumpy, worn out couch. "He'll be out of the bathroom in a minute."

Red could hear the water running from beyond the partially opened bathroom door. His eyes caught sight of the infant who appeared fast asleep in the old let-out couch which served as a bed. The soiled blanket, which covered the baby, was also protecting part of the floor.

The door of the bathroom squeaked as Bob, a scrawnily built man with dope-glazed eyes, entered the room.

"Hi, dude," he greeted Red. "Look man, I haven't made up yet, but things will be cool in a few days."

Red raised himself from the uncomfortable couch. "That's what you told us two weeks ago, man. Monk told me to tell you he couldn't wait any longer."

Bob was perspiring quite heavily as he spoke. "The stuff ain't good as it usta be, man. I'm having trouble moving it."

Red's expression changed immediately. "Monk figured you might come up with a stall."

Bob's big-eyed woman had moved to the dilapidated let-out couch to sit on the edge of it.

"Look, Daddy," Bob said, "I'm not trying to rip . . ."

by Randolph Harris

Red let go with an unexpected right cross which caught Bob flush on the chin. "You've used the stuff yourself, you junkie bastard. How much do you have left? Huh? Answer me! How much do you have left?"

Bob's frail body lay sprawled between the much used sitting couch and the make-shift bed. His saucer-eyed girl friend readily sprang to her feet. But she was distracted by a tearful outcry from the bed.

Bob rolled over, shaking the cobwebs from his skull. He was instantly rewarded with a kick from Red's blunt-toed shoes. Real hard it was.

"Where's the rest of that junk, you prick?" Red's face was now flushed crimson.

Bob's hysterical girl friend, now holding the baby in her arms, screamed, "Oh, my God, don't kill him. He's sick! Do you hear me? He's sick!" Her face was wildly distorted, which obviously added fear within her crying child.

It was then that the lava gushed, erupting from Bob's lips, while his skeleton frame jerked in convulsive fashion, and blood streamed in lumps from his nostrils.

"Oh! My God!" The frail lady's eyes targeted on the old kitchen knife which rested idly on the worn table.

With her left hand grasped tightly around the

THE BLACK CONNECTION

infant in her arms, and extending her right hand, she instinctively clutched the dirty utensil and plunged it forcefully into Red's spine.

There was a look of sudden surprise, though quite grotesque, on Red's slender face as he seemed to arch his back and turn, before he did a zombie step and fell.

The moon-eyed girl had wrapped both arms around her child and backed against the dingy wall. Red was on the floor. He had coughed twice as he clawed for the snub-nosed .38 which was still held snugly in his belt. Clearly, he was using his dying strength to aim it toward the girl and child who were plastered against the wall in shock.

Her eyes saw Red's fingers as they made snail-like movements, but somehow she could not budge. She closed her terror-filled eyes and held a tighter grasp on her tiny offspring. Then she heard a thud. She forced open her eyes, and there before her lay two bodies, though only one of them was still breathing.

It was the next morning when Sonya, Monk's wife, excitedly aroused him. "Oscar! Oscar! Wake up!" she exclaimed. "It's Red. He's dead. Wake up!"

Monk responded with a puzzled look, sleepily reaching for the newspaper that Sonya was nerv-

by Randolph Harris

ously pointing at him.

"What is it?"

"It's Red. See, there's his name and address, right there." Sonya had one hand grasping the paper. With the other, she was pointing at the print.

"Ain't this a bitch!" Monk was now sitting up. He wiped his eyes, as if to see better. Then, he wiped them again, as if in disbelief. He stretched for the phone, then hurriedly dialed. "Hello, Charlie? Have you seen the paper? Red got himself offed. Oh, yeah, I forgot about that. Well, when you leave the airport, meet me at the bar." Monk hung up.

"Run me some bath water, Sonya. I forgot that I told Charlie to take Bonito to the airport this morning."

Monk Davis continued to read the paper. The article explained that Sylvia Jones had stabbed Willie (Red) Morris while he, Morris, was attempting to rob her common-law husband, Robert Smith.

It went on to state that the police were holding Miss Jones for murder, while Robert Smith was being confined as a material witness. Monk threw the paper to the floor in disgust.

"Robbery! Ain't that a bitch? Why, that crumb-bum whore. She'll walk out of the courtroom scot-free. But she'd better book passage to the moon; her *and* that dope-fiend man of hers." Monk was talking to Sonya, who had just entered the room.

"Your bath water's ready. Do you really think they'll let her go?"

Monk was on the side of the bed sliding into his robe when he said, "You're damn right they will. But if they both know like I know, they'd stay in jail. Damn! It's warm in here. Have you got the air-conditioner turned off?"

"I told you yesterday," Sonya responded, "that I called the repair man. I don't know what happened to him."

"Well, call him again. It's stuffier than hell in here." Monk continued to the bathroom enclosure.

Monk was sitting in the 808 Club as Dumont entered and topped the stool next to him.

"Did Bonito get off all right?" Monk asked, as he raised his glass of beer.

"Aw, yeah," Dumont answered. "Everything went off beautifully. Say, man, what about Red. I know you're not forgetting about it."

"No, I'm not. But right now there are other things that must be taken care of." Monk seemed to be pondering as he continued. "I'm going to meet some of the 'Black Angels' crowd upstairs in

by Randolph Harris

about twenty minutes." Monk was looking at his watch.

"Really! What's happening with them?"

"Aw, they've formed some kind of street gang and they think we should pay them a protection fee for our pushers to operate in the neighborhood."

"You're not going for it, are you?"

"Shit, naw. Once we start paying them, you know what that would mean?"

"Yeah, and anyway, they're nothing but a lotta young punks from what I've heard," remarked Dumont, as he lit his cigarette.

"But you can't play them too cheap. They can be really dangerous." Monk glanced at his diamond-dial again. "I'd better get upstairs. I've got a little surprise fixed up for them."

"Will you need me?"

"Not necessarily. Why?"

"Aw, I promised Jimmy I'd buy him some boxing gloves for his birthday, which is tomorrow."

"That's right. I forgot all about your kid brother. How is he?"

"He's okay. He's only sixteen, and thinks he's another Joe Louis." Dumont was smiling.

"Naw, I don't think I'll need you. I've got Nick and Buba upstairs and I'm sure they can take care of things."

THE BLACK CONNECTION

"You're not kidding. Those two can take care of anything. Okay, I'll see you when I come from downtown." Saying that, Dumont departed.

Monk finised his beer. A round, chubby man and a rather statuesque lady were dancing to the beat of the vendor music. Monk stepped around them, went out of the bar and opened the wooden door which led to the apartment above.

He joined two men who were already inside. Nick, the first man, was a fair replica of a giant: 6'5" tall, and weighing two hundred-ninety pounds. A little flesh, the necessary bones, but most of it muscle. His head was shaven clean and his small eyes peered from an ebony background. His appearance was amazingly stalwart.

The second man, Buba, was 6'4" tall with a brown complexion, and his weight was two hundred and sixty-five pounds. His flowery sport shirt travelled down into brown checkered slacks. His appearance loomed equally as sturdy as Nick's.

Monk sat side-legged on the old dresser with one foot touching the floor. "I thought they'd be here by now." Monk pinned his watch again.

"What's that?" Nick asked, twisting his head toward the door. Sounds from the creaking steps had floated into the room.

"It's probably them," Monk answered. "All right, you two know what to do."

by Randolph Harris

There came a knock at the door. "Come on in. It's open!" Monk shouted.

Through the door appeared two youthful-looking boys—sixteen or seventeen years old, no more.

"Have a seat." Monk pointed to the old couch.

The two youths, one light-complexioned, tall, with a rather bushy Afro; the other medium height, dark brown and with a similar Afro, both sat down.

Nick and Buba, each with their arms folded, took statue-like positions on each side of Monk.

"Now tell me what's on your minds, fellows." Monk was quite blunt.

"Well, man," the tall youth answered, "it's like we said before. You dudes are getting big scratch out of our neighborhood, and we want a piece of it."

"Yeah!" the shorter youth echoed. "We like bread too, man."

Monk looked down at the two youths who were sitting on the old couch, then said, "Well, fellows, I'm going out for a few minutes. I'm sure Nick and Buba here will give you something." Monk spun around and walked out the door.

The two youths were instantly alerted. The tall, light-complexioned boy sprang from the couch and produced a six-inch blade knife that had been

THE BLACK CONNECTION

strapped next to his wrist by a narrow rubber band.

The shorter and much darker lad sprang atop the couch while reaching to his left sock; the familiar click identified the glistening blade before it appeared, protruding from the boy's fist. He was in a crouch as though ready to leap. The tall youth was also hunched forward with his knife poised, and he was flicking it toward Nick, who had reached for and grabbed a chair. Nick drew back the chair as if to bat a home-run. There was a tremendous crash, and the chair met bones and flesh.

As the knife flew from the lad's hand, the youth's body flew against the wall. Clearly it was no contest.

The smaller youth had leaped from the old couch. He was trying to make it to the door. Buba, however, had other ideas as he feinted at the youth who made a lunge with the knife. It was the young man's last voluntary act.

Buba sidestepped the intended thrust, and grabbed the small arm. The boy's body resembled a doll as it was propelled through air in circus-like fashion. Had anyone witnessed the ensuing mayhem, they would have been forced to call homicide. However, an hour later, a laundry man making his daily calls in the rear of the building put through the emergency call when he found the

by Randolph Harris

two bodies bleeding and stirring. It was truly a gory sight.

When the ambulance arrived to transfer the victims to the hospital, a crowd had gathered in the alley. Amongst the frowning onlookers were agents Danny Gruff and Sidney Miller.

It was the next day and Jimmy Dumont, sixteen-year-old brother of Charles, was displaying his new boxing gloves to his little friend Sammy, who was seventeen.

"I guess you're on your way to the gym now," Sammy asked.

"Yeah," answered Jimmy. "This will be the first chance I've had to try out my new gloves. Want to come along?"

"Naw, I'm going to the pool hall."

Jimmy Dumont was a lanky boy about five-feet-ten. Sammy was a chubby five-feet-eight. Both boys wore blue denims as they quickened their strides and dashed across 47th Street at Calumet Avenue. The pool hall was only two doors from the corner.

"See ya' this evening when you come from the gym."

"Okay." Jimmy continued toward the L-train station, his transportation to the gym.

At the same time, Monk was at his apartment talking to Charles Dumont on the phone.

THE BLACK CONNECTION

"Yeah, Nick and Buba took care of those punks. think one of the kids had to have surgery."

"That," Dumont pointed out, "should straighten them out for a while."

"Yeah, for a while, but like I said, they can be dangerous. You know there's quite a gang of them."

"Say, man, what about that run we were supposed to make?"

"That's what I called to tell ya'. Sonya is packing my things now. You and I will leave together—she'll fly over later. I've already talked to Santino. He told me Bonito should be in Detroit tonight."

"That's crazy!" Dumont sounded elated. "I haven't taken a trip since I've been home. What time do we leave?"

"It's ten after one now. I'll pick you up at two o'clock. I've already made our reservations and the plane won't leave until three."

"Okay, I'll be ready."

It was ten minutes after two when Agents Gruff and Miller parked facing south at 52nd on Cottage Grove Avenue. Washington Park sprawled to the right of them. The wide spread of grass, dotted with trees and hedges, faced the newly built high-rise apartment building, and out front a black car was waiting: Dumont resided here.

by Randolph Harris

"Well," said Agent Gruff to his partner, "it looks like the Monk is about to take a trip."

"Yeah, but it must be a short one. He only put one bag in the car trunk. That's that guy Beany driving, isn't it?"

"Yep," Gruff answered, squinting a distance and recognizing the processed head behind the wheel of the waiting car.

Shortly, Dumont, dressed in an Edwardian-tailored blue suit, and accompanied by Monk who wore a green sport coat and brown slacks, came bouncing from the apartment building entrance. Dumont was carrying a plaid leather-trimmed folding bag. They were in a hurry.

Beany, a medium height brown-skinned young man, noticed them coming and got out of the car to open the car trunk. Swiftly the black car drove away.

The black sedan driven by Beany had headed north on the Dan Ryan Expressway. Agents Gruff and Miller in a dark brown car followed at a safe distance. At least ten car lengths.

"If we had known this, we could have made arrangements to stick with them. They're headed to the airport and that's for sure," Gruff said, as his eyes traced the black sedan.

"Maybe if we dispatch the chief we can have them met and tailed on the other end."

THE BLACK CONNECTION

"Good idea," Gruff answered, as he reached for the dispatch phone on the car dashboard.

Along with other traffic the two cars left the expressway and followed the airport entourage.

"The chief," Gruff said after speaking on the phone, "said to find out their destination and call him back right away. He'll call ahead their descriptions and have a tail waiting for them. Say, do we still have that sham bag in the car trunk?"

"Yeah, the last time we used it was to tail that woman at the train station," Miller replied.

"Good."

The airport was crowded as usual as Beany let out Monk and Dumont with their luggage. Then Beany drove away.

Agent Sidney Miller parked the dark brown car, retrieved the light tan sham bag from the car trunk, and he and Agent Gruff followed Monk and Dumont inside the terminal.

Oscar (Monk) Davis hurried to the reservation counter while looking at his watch. When he left, neither he nor Dumont noticed the slightly grey-haired gentleman approach the reservation counter and flash a folder. If they had, he would have surely been mistaken as just another customer who was presenting his identification in order to confirm his reservation. Had Monk or Dumont continued to look, they may have become alerted

by Randolph Harris

had they seen the reservation clerk turn his head in their direction and then look down at the sheet of paper in front of him.

Agent Miller sauntered to the nearest phone and relayed the destination of the two Black men. Then he joined Agent Gruff who was furtively watching Monk and Dumont at Gate 15 to make sure that the two Black men would take their intended flight.

Later that night a tall youth with a bushy Afro and his arm in a sling was in a rundown basement apartment with five other youths, telling them about he and his companion's unfortunate accident.

"Aw, they were big dudes, man. The doctors said that Odell would be in the hospital for at least two weeks." The young boy gingerly felt his bandaged arm.

A thin-faced dark lad spoke up. "Those dope-pushing motherfuckers think we're a bunch of punks!" He glanced over at one of the four and said, "Railhead, you and Punchy go with Ronnie. He'll point them out. Then we'll see how they like some heat."

The young boys filed out of the basement heading toward an old green station wagon which, from an outward appearance, had long since seen better days. However, considering the stolen parts

THE BLACK CONNECTION

assembled beneath the battered hood, it performed surprisingly well as the boys drove away.

Nick and Buba were standing at the bar of the 808 Club. Buba was popping his fingers in time with the vendor music, Beany was in one of the only two wall booths making smooching love to a buxom brown-skinned Afro wearer.

"Say, man," Nick said to Buba, "let's split outside and grab a smoke."

"I ain't got nothing, have you?" Buba was looking back at Nick.

"Yeah, I got a joint that I rolled before I left home."

"Come on."

The two over-sized men moved along the row of bar stools and went out the door.

"Come on, let's sit in Beany's car while he's busy inside with Betty."

Nick followed Buba's suggestion and the two giant men entered the black sedan which had earlier made the airport trip.

They never noticed the old station wagon as it circled the block for the second time. On the second revolution it slowed as it neared the black sedan, and inside the station wagon a flame flared and illuminated the figures in the rear. When the battered station wagon came alongside the black sedan, a small arm appeared and tossed the flaming

by Randolph Harris

bottle. Then, another black arm appeared from the rear of the station wagon and threw another bottle which appeared to have a flaming mouth. The sound of the antique station wagon speeding away was drowned out by the thunderous explosion.

A shrieking cry was heard from within the flaming black sedan. People in the apartments above were aroused by the dancing fire below. The door of the black car seemed to burst open and a massive figure of a man stumbled out, writhing and twisting as flames engulfed his body.

The street traffic made a wide arch as perplexity engulfed the entire block. From a distance an approaching siren could be heard. But to the viewers of this sudden holocaust, it was obvious that the fire wagon was a bit tardy.

chapter 3

AT DETROIT'S METROPOLITAN AIRPORT, a slight haze had marred what had been a lovely day. Monk and Charles Dumont had retrieved their luggage and were standing outside, about to hail a cab.

A few moments later they were on their way to the inner-city. Their red and white cab rolled along Willow Run Road. Farther back, a dark blue car contained two Black agents, Roscoe E. Brown and Wesley Phillips. They had been assigned the task of observing the two cab passengers for the duration of the outsiders' stay in Detroit.

A shower of rain had begun to fall as the cab stopped in front of a downtown Detroit hotel. Before leaving Chicago, Monk had called and made reservations for two choice rooms with a connecting bath. The two newly arrived guests strolled

THE BLACK CONNECTION

through the spacious lobby as if they were business executives. This would have been an established fact if one could have counted the astronomical funds concealed within Monk's traveling bag.

Once retired within their separate rooms, Monk walked through the dividing bath and entered Charlie Dumont's room.

"Well, how do you like it, Charlie?" Monk sprawled onto the velvety blue couch. "It's a long way from that prison cell, ain't it?"

"You're damn right it is," Dumont answered as he treaded over the plush deep blue carpeting and inspected the elaborate furnishings. "Shit, these rooms probably cost more per day than my apartment cost all month."

Monk, however, never verified Charlie's imagination. "This is how those whiteys live every day, man," Monk said. "I made up my mind a long time ago that I was going to get out of that stinking ghetto. If you stick with me, Charlie, you'll get out, too. Come on, I'll show you something."

The two men walked through the connecting bathroom and entered Monk's room, which was laid out in a fabulous decor of green and white. A king-sized bed covered a portion of the deep shag green carpet. The patter of rain could be heard on the other side of the window which was shielded by the expensive green and white drapes.

by Randolph Harris

Monk went to his traveling bag and removed a black leather wallet. He pulled the zipper and exposed the contents.

Charlie viewed the bundles of green currency and let out a whistle. "Motherfucker! I've never seen so much bread at one time. We must be buying all the stuff in the world."

"Hell no, man. That's only a hundred gee's. But it's going to buy us five kees that can be cut three times. Bonito and some of his people will be in town tonight. Then we'll go to the races over in Canada."

At that moment, the telephone rang. Monk sauntered over to the night table and lifted the receiver. "Hello . . . Hi, baby, I figured it was you. What time are you leaving? . . . What?" The shock in Monk's voice forced Charles Dumont to look up. Monk's face was frozen in anguish. "Both of them?" Monk asked into the phone. "Okay. Come to room 819. Don't stop at the desk. Just take the elevator and come up. Oh, yeah, don't bring any bags. And wear one of your wigs."

Putting the receiver down Monk turned and, without looking at Dumont, said, "Nick and Buba are dead."

"You're kidding!" With a frown on his face, Dumont waited for Monk to continue.

"Damn it!" Monk kicked his traveling bag,

THE BLACK CONNECTION

which lay openly on the floor. "I told them to watch out; those punks could be dangerous!"

Monk pulled the cord and the heavily hung drapes parted. His eyes focused down on the crawling traffic and the minute pedestrians. But Dumont could sense that Monk's mind was not on the hustling activities below.

"What are we going to do, Oscar?"

Still staring as though in a trance, Monk answered, "We're going to make those punks wish they were never born. We'll get our business cleared up tonight and be back there tomorrow."

"How did it happen?"

"Aw, they were sitting in Beany's car and got two Molotovs."

"Damn," Charlie remarked. "That's a helluva way to be taken out."

The brief rain had stopped and dusk was captivating the city. Street lights showed dimly through the haze and pinpoints from the moving vehicles below seemed like wandering cat eyes. Monk turned from the panoramic window. "I'm going to lay down and relax until Bonito calls or Sonya comes in."

Dumont knew that Monk wanted to think. He patted him on the shoulder, then walked through the dividing bath into his own room and closed the door.

by Randolph Harris

After completing a bit of clandestine research, Agents Brown and Phillips tried to rent a room near the two men whom they had been assigned to observe. However, their efforts proved fruitless, since all rooms across and near 818-819 were presently occupied. Fearing they might alert Monk and Dumont, and realizing the close relationship so frequently acquired between big tippers and hotel employees, the two Black agents took up a vigil across the street in their parked car.

Agent Roscoe E. Brown, a tall, light brown-skinned man was a graduate of U.C.L.A. Thirty-five years old, he had been on the varsity football team, and had taken courses in criminology. He later joined the Narcotics Bureau.

Agent Phillips was 5'10", had formerly been with the Detroit Police Department, and his dark brown complexion showed curving lines of experience. He was forty-one years old and a veteran of ten years with the Bureau of Narcotics.

"Well, Phil," Agent Brown said exasperatedly, "this looks like another bowling night shot to hell."

"Aw, what difference does it make? You'd probably have to buy the beer anyway."

"Listen to you. I seem to recall you were going to take somebody to the movies tonight. Right?"

"Hell, yes, but how can you make plans on this

crummy job?"

"Who're you crapping? You'd be lost without it."

The two agents looked at each other, smiled, and settled back.

It was three hours later. Agent Brown was slouched down in the car seat, hat pulled down over his eyes. Agent Phillips' eyes were targeted on the hotel entrance when a cab released a tall, attractive and very shapely Negro woman with blazing red hair.

"Those wigs certainly are popular these days."

"Humph." Brown never moved his head.

Another hour passed and the same redheaded lady reappeared through the hotel entrance, only now she was escorted by a middle-aged white man who was dapperly dressed and carried an attache case. He was dark-complexioned like a Greek, a Puerto Rican, or perhaps even an Italian. They entered a car which was parked near the hotel entrance. The white man got behind the steering wheel and drove away.

"It's getting to the point where you can't tell a whore from a lady," Phillips murmured.

Agent Brown sat up in his seat, pushed his hat straight, and remarked boringly, "All right. What did she look like?"

"Aw, she was probably just another hooker

by Randolph Harris

coming to meet her sponsor."

"Say, look," Brown twisted his head toward the hotel entrance.

The two agents caught sight of Oscar (Monk) Davis and Charles Dumont entering a green sedan which was parked about two spaces from where the lady and her companion's car had been.

"Now that's odd," Phillips said. "A white guy parked that car there about an hour ago."

They saw Dumont slide behind the steering wheel and the car left the curb. The agents immediately took up the trail, though with ultimate caution. The green car led them down Woodward Boulevard, then turned left and headed east.

Shortly, the green car led them into several rows of cars which were barely moving. Phillips, who was driving, nodded his head. "Well, I'll be . . . It looks like we're leaving the country, ole chappie."

Brown could not miss the huge sign, white letters on a green background with an arrow underneath pointing straight ahead: *WINDSOR AHEAD.*

"It looks like our friends have decided to take in the night trotting races over in Canada," Brown said.

"Well, you know we lose all jurisdiction once we cross the border," Phillips filled in.

"What difference does it make? We're on a recon mission anyway."

THE BLACK CONNECTION

"Yeah, I guess you're right."

The agents' car was issued through the shuttle with the rest of the vehicles and they found themselves in Canada. After a few careful maneuvers to avoid being observed—though there was little chance with so many cars heading for the same destination—the agents saw a gigantic glowing red sign which read, *WINDSOR RACEWAY*.

Phillips had placed the dark blue car directly behind the green sedan and the long rows of cars were pulling into the wide and spacious parking areas. When Monk and Dumont alighted from their car, the two Black men who parked next to them appeared as just some other racetrack fans.

People rushed from the parking areas toward the racetrack and the loudspeakers announcing the upcoming race could clearly be heard. Racing fans were unfolding newspapers and purchasing programs as Monk and Dumont entered the gate.

The agents followed the two Black men through the shuffling crowd and saw them go up the stairs and take two seats inside the stadium. Brown and Phillips did not take seats. From a distance they merely observed. An obese lady and her male companion took two seats next to Monk and Dumont. Their massive physiques partially blocked the agents' view. The two agents were at an obscured vantage point, so they moved.

by Randolph Harris

"The horses are near the post!"

The loudspeakers blared as the horses paraded in front of the bobbing sulkys. Drivers with jerseys of glowing colors and wide spread legs steered their charges postward. Phillips, who appeared very interested in the program he held, was actually viewing the two suspects when he spied Monk rise from the seat and leave. The agent couldn't help noticing the fine tailoring of Monk's tan sportcoat. Agent Phillips cautiously followed the Monk. Agent Brown remained steadfast; as did Dumont.

"The horses are at the post." The announcer spoke again.

Monk quickened his steps. He descended the stairs, weaved through the excited crowd and approached the fifty dollar bettor's window. The teller punched off two tickets.

"And they're off!" The loudspeaker blasted. An over-eager bettor raced down the stairs and bumped into Agent Phillips, uttering a fleeting apology and lost himself in the crowd. Phillips readjusted himself, Monk was gone! Coincidence? It had to be. Phillips craned his neck and scanned the mezzanine. Monk, the light tan sportcoat; both were gone.

The agent raced up the stairs and back into the stands. Dumont was standing, cheering and alone.

The sulkys were being drawn into the stretch.

THE BLACK CONNECTION

Fans were yelling. Monk was nowhere. The tiring trotters were within inches of the wire. The crowd reached its highest tempo. No Monk. Realizing the inescapable fact that Monk would eventually rejoin his companion, Phillips dejectedly rejoined Agent Brown.

"I goofed."

"Don't the best of us?"

"The damn guy just vanished."

"It is odd," Brown agreed.

The crowd momentarily recovered from the past race.

"The horses are on the track for the next race!" the loudspeaker bellowed.

"I've got a shitty feeling about this thing."

"Now look, Phil, don't let it bug you. The guy's gonna return."

"But, Roscoe, you know damn well that something is happening this very minute that we should know about."

"The horses will reach the post in five minutes." Again the nasal announcer spoke.

"Look!"

"Well, I'll be a son-of-a-bitch! Roscoe, we missed the big pitch." Agent Phillips was scanning the crowd.

Monk and the tall, shapely redhead were coming up the stairs. They were talking and smiling to each

by Randolph Harris

other. From his perched seat, Dumont had spied them. Now he was smiling.

"Damn it, it's her," Phillips said.

"Who's the dame?" Brown asked. "Who is she?"

"She's the same one," Phillips remarked. "The one I saw at the hotel. She rode away with a white dude."

"This is a bitch! Damn racehorse bettors." Phillips was referring to the man who had bumped into him and caused the agent to lose sight of his quarry. Monk and his red-topped wife joined Dumont, who moved over a seat and allowed Sonya to sit in the middle.

"The chief told us only to observe and report, but, damn it, this whole thing smells of Narco."

"Phil, I think you've hit it. You say she left the hotel with a white guy, huh?"

"Yeah," Phillips gestured with his hand. "About so tall he was."

"This is a damn good place for a pass all right. Say, how about the other car that she and the white guy came in? I'll bet a year's salary that's where the stuff is stashed."

"The horses are at the post!" The crowd was alerted by the loudspeaker. Sonya, Monk's wife, rose from her seat, then turned and kissed Monk on his cheek. Dumont waved his program at her.

"Phil!" Agent Brown was looking over the edge

THE BLACK CONNECTION

of his newspaper. "She's leaving."

"Yeah," Phillips answered, grudgingly. "I'd like to tail her, but our orders were to watch and report on those two sharpies. We'd feel like shit if the lady wasn't even connected."

"You're right, of course. But, Phil, you know how I get a feeling about these things."

"I wish we had another car." Agent Wesley Phillips looked dejected.

"And they're off!" The crowd stood. Sonya descended the stairs.

"Maybe I should tail her and get the license plate numbers anyway."

"Good idea, Roscoe."

Sonya's tall figure, with her dark grey dress, wiggled down the stairs, out the gate, and into the parking lot. She zigzagged through the rows of parked cars and finally settled on a black sedan with Michigan license plates.

Agent Brown, well experienced in the art of shadowing, was only three cars away as he pretended to have a weak bladder. He jotted down the description and license plate numbers of the car. Sonya pulled away in the car, and Brown retraced his steps into the racetrack.

The last race was coming up. Monk and Dumont had left to avoid the last minute traffic. As they came out on the United States side, Monk said,

by Randolph Harris

"Well, things went smooth, just like Bonito said they would."

"Yeah," Dumont answered. "Renting those cars was a damn good idea."

"The whole idea was old man Santino's. It's like Bonito said. 'The old man is smart'."

"It didn't take you and Sonya long to make the switch, did it?"

"Naw, as soon as I got my tickets in the fifth race, I met her outside in the parking lot, just as Bonito had planned it. But you know what? I had the damndest feeling, like somebody was tailing me."

"Just your imagination."

"Damn right, it was. Otherwise, I wouldn't be here now!" The two men laughed.

"Where is Sonya now?" Dumont asked.

Monk looked at his watch. "She should be at the airport. Her plane leaves in eighteen minutes."

"What about that rented car that Bonito had delivered to the hotel?"

"Why, she'll check that in at the airport."

"Oh, I dig. That's why you told her to leave her bags at home."

"Beautiful, ain't it? Now, she's got a bag, and man—whatta bag!" Dumont, who was driving, held the wheel with his left hand and stuck out his right, palm up. Monk slapped it.

THE BLACK CONNECTION

The rented car rolled into the downtown section of Detroit. Towering buildings engulfed it.

"The hotel has a parking lot in the rear. Use it," Monk said.

"Beautiful." Dumont turned the corner.

After parking the car, the two dope dealers were back in Monk's room. Dumont was on the green couch, head at one end and ankle over ankle propped up on the other armrest. Monk was dialing the phone.

"You haven't had much fun since you've been out of that joint. I think I'll get you some choice company."

"That sounds mellow, baby."

"Hello? Monk . . . well, you know I had to see you before I left. Yeah . . . . uh, huh . . . bring a friend for my friend . . . Beautiful." Monk hung up.

"Are they coming over?"

"Remember this, Charlie. Very few broads refuse to see you when they know you've got long bread."

"Man, I know what'cha mean."

Monk uncradled the phone again. "Hello . . . Room Service?"

It was an hour later. Dumont walked through the adjoining bathroom in his multi-shaded blue

by Randolph Harris

robe.

"Damn, man. What happened to those broads?"

"Run some cold water on your joint, man. They'll be here. Come on, fix yourself a drink and forget about your hard." Monk pointed at the bottle of scotch which was surrounded by ice and a multitude of liquors and mixes. It was all top quality—the best.

Shortly, the phone rang. Monk picked up the receiver. "Yeah . . . okay. Send them up."

"They showed, huh?"

"Yeah, they showed, man. The broads are not crazy. They want some bread."

In another moment, the door buzzer sounded. Without hesitating, Monk opened it. "What do ya know, baby?" Monk greeted a tall, shapely Amazon-looking chick. She wasn't as tall as Monk, but it looked as if she could have given him a real good wrestling match, in bed or elsewhere.

The other young lady was just the opposite: small-boned, petite, brown, with comparatively large eyes. Oh, yeah, she also was quite shapely. After everyone was introduced, Monk uttered a demanding question. "All right, let's see what those bodies look like."

Marie, the buxom lady, said, "You've seen this one before, daddy, but it's been a long time." The other girl, Lucy, just smiled.

THE BLACK CONNECTION

If the agents had been listening an hour later, they would have sworn Dumont was committing mayhem. There were outcries and moans floating from Dumont's room that suggested anything but sex. Professional whore that she was, Lucy had never been put through such an ordeal.

The positions that the small woman's body was forced to submit to were some of which she never would have imagined. Whether on her back or on her stomach, Dumont would definitely find an opening. And then, to her surprise, he would find two openings at the same time. There were often times when their bodies would resemble a pretzel. In all of these gymnastic variations, Lucy would find it most difficult to breathe; she was simply stopped up.

When the ordeal was over, Lucy confronted the bathroom mirror and was amazed at the black and blue marks that showed across her small body. Without any doubt, Dumont was an out and out sadist.

Meanwhile Monk, on the other hand, was more reserved in his sexual endeavors. When he was lying on his back, Marie would assuredly be sitting in his lap as though she was riding a horse. At other times, she would be bent over on her knees, and Monk would appear to be the bouncing jockey. However, this was the most puzzling thing of all;

by Randolph Harris

during these entire posture exchanges, Marie was constantly chewing gum.

It was early the following morning when the plane carrying the two dope dealers departed from Detroit's Metropolitan Airport. Clouds resembling puffs of smoke umbrella'd the plane which was now pointed for Chicago. Monk and Dumont settled back in their seats.

"I made a call to New York before we left," Monk said. "I sent for some dudes to take care of that 'Angel' bunch."

"Aw, man, we should be able to handle those youngbloods."

"That's just it. We'll have our hands full distributing our stuff—and I don't want no static of any kind. You see, man, this thing could develop into a little war, and that'll be bad if it gets back to Bonito or the ole man."

"Yeah, I get it. We let some out-of-town guys do the job and we'll all have alibis."

"That's right. Now that Red is gone, there's only eight of us left. But whenever things jump off, you and I will be out of town. It looks beautiful out there, doesn't it?" Monk had turned and was looking at the passing clouds.

"Yes, it does. But say, man, how're we gonna be sure who offed Nick and Buba?" Dumont asked.

"Aw, that's easy. Beany and the rest of the guys

THE BLACK CONNECTION

probably know already. You know, Charlie, there's a lot of those young dudes using stuff. And for a twenty-five dollar pack, they'd tell on their mamas."

"Yeah, I guess you're right."

The stewardess was offering coffee. Dumont took a cup, Monk refused. "We should be landing soon." Monk was glancing at his watch.

"Man, these jets are crazy! Look how steady this coffee is."

"That's right, you had never been on one before you went to the joint, had you?"

"Hell naw, man, I was lucky to ride on a bus! Shit, Oscar, you know that."

"Yeah," Monk answered, rather musingly. "You know, Charlie, this is a long way from the old neighborhood where we were kids."

"You're damn right it is!" Dumont sipped his coffee.

The stewardess advised everyone to fasten their seatbelts. The plane was about to land.

A while later Sonya, no longer wearing her red wig, was seen driving away from the airport in Monk's dark grey Oldsmobile. Monk was sitting in the front seat, Dumont was sitting in the rear.

As Sonya turned the car into the Dan Ryan Expressway, another car, farther back and un-

by Randolph Harris

noticed, was following. Its two occupants were a prematurely grey-haired guy, and a man with a ruddy pock-marked face. His name was Miller.

In the dark grey Olds, Monk asked Sonya, "How was your trip?"

"Okay," Sonya answered. "Everything was cool. I checked the bag through like you said, then picked it up after the plane landed. No trouble at all. I was wondering if you guys would be back in time for the wakes."

"What time are they?" Monk asked.

"Eight-thirty. The wakes and the funeral will be held together," Sonya answered.

"Counting Red, that's three righteous dudes who've been taken out," Dumont remarked.

"Yeah, but they'll be accounted for." Monk was looking at the fleeting scenery as he answered.

That night, while the wakes were in progress, a plane was about to take off from New York's LaGuardia Airport. Two medium-built Black men were amongst the passengers. Neither of the men carried luggage, and neither of them had checked any baggage. Both men carried round-trip tickets.

The wakes were over and Monk was speaking to the two New York visitors who had recently arrived at the 808 Club by cab. They were upstairs over the tavern, and the small group included

THE BLACK CONNECTION

Dumont.

"They have a basement hangout over on 55th Street," Monk said, "and they usually gather there after the 2 o'clock taverns close."

The tallest of the two New Yorkers spoke up. "What do you mean, the two o'clock taverns?"

"Well," Monk explained while Dumont, who was sitting on the couch, looked on "here in Chicago, the taverns have two closing hours, one at two o'clock, and the last ones close at four."

"I dig." The man who had asked the question nodded his head.

Monk handed the man a pack of money with a wrapper around it. "The balance will be delivered to you tomorrow by someone in New York after I know the job is done."

Shortly, the two out-of-towners were seen entering a car which had been supplied by Monk. The shortest of the two men carried a package.

It was only moments later when Monk and Dumont entered the dark grey Oldsmobile and drove away. Monk said, "We'll be in Gary, Indiana in about twenty minutes. Everybody hangs out at Morris' place, so that's where we'll go."

"So this is what you meant when you said we'd be out of town, huh?"

"Right. It's only thirty miles away, but there'll be plenty of witnesses who'll swear that we were

by Randolph Harris

there."

The dark grey Olds rolled through Washington Park and came out on Stony Island Avenue. It was last seen going up the expressway ramp.

chapter 4

THE SHORTER of the out-of-town strangers got out of the car, while his taller companion remained behind the steering wheel. The man walked stealthily around the side of the building, which was situated on 51st and Prairie Avenue. He stopped, leaned over, and listened at the basement window. His ears were assaulted by rhythmical sounds which came from a small radio. There was also a mixture of voices, though these were less vibrant. The short man crept back along the side of the rundown structure and stopped at the time-worn door. He heard the toot of a car horn, looked toward the car which held his taller companion, then backed into the shadows of the darkened enclosure.

THE BLACK CONNECTION

A man and woman got out of a car and entered the building next door. The short man bent over out of the shadows and continued his furtive movements. From under his coat, he removed a package. It was the same package he had held when he and his associate had left the 808 Club.

He placed the cigar box-sized package at the foot of the door, produced his cigarette lighter from his pocket, and lit the small candle-like stem. The small man now moved with the speed of an athlete.

The deteriorating entrance to the basement was momentarily illuminated. Then, squealing tires from the fast departing automobile were instantly drowned out by the thunderously loud explosion. Glass and concrete crumpled and the mixture of clutter shattered the night silence.

The tenants in the first floor apartments let out screams of shock. Some were cries of anguish. Windows from above and around the flaming rubble were hastily opened to display inquiring heads.

A scrawny figure staggered from the flaming shambles and collapsed on the cluttered basement steps. It was a raging holocaust! The car containing the two out-of-town men rolled to 52nd Street and turned right, then poured into Indiana Avenue. They parked the car in the middle of the block and

by Randolph Harris

got out. The two men walked back to 51st Street and hailed a cab. While the cab was going along the expressway, the tall man told the cab driver: "Ain't no need to rush, man; our plane won't leave for two more hours."

The cab driver nodded from his glass-enclosed cubicle.

At the time of the explosion, Oscar (Monk) Davis and Charlie Dumont were thirty miles away in Gary, Indiana at Morris' Place. They were hosting a rather hilarious crowd to the establishment's choice of drinks. It was definitely a happy late hour scene. Ladies of the evening had retired from their nightly chores. Colorfully dressed men were posing for their spouses. The vendor was giving out with fast beats as a mini-skirted girl gyrated in the center of the floor.

Fancy drinks lined the bar as the two big spenders made their presence known. If an inquiring guest should happen to ask, he or she would lucidly be told, "Why, tha's bigtime Monk and his man, Charlie Dumont."

Thus, Monk's intended mission was now accomplished.

The following day the neighborhood was saturated with talk of the horrible bombing disaster. The newspapers carried columns decrying the

THE BLACK CONNECTION

violence of street gangs. Five youths had been killed from the bomb blast. One sixteen-year-old boy who was found outside the shattered basement was declared in serious condition. A lady and her two-year-old daughter who slept in a bedroom above the basement were hospitalized and both were announced as critical. Clearly, rival street gang retaliation was the expressed cause.

Police and firemen were informed by nearby neighbors that the obscure basement had long been a street gang hangout. One old lady in particular wasn't shy with her tongue. Her chestnut-brown face cracked as she said, "Lawd! The goin's-on that usta happen in that basement! Why, they'd stay down thar till the wee-hours of the morning!"

Harry (Big Jim) Sanders, the Black alderman of the ward, was among the bewildered spectators. A dark-skinned, paunchy and seemingly homely man, Jim had long been rumored to be an obedient servant of the powerful downtown city council.

Television crews were busily at work and reporters were asking for brief interviews. Alerted by the possibliity of making political gain, Big Jim ostensibly went about stealing the well attended scene. A reporter was holding the microphone. "I have indeed brought the street gang situation to the attention of the council," Big Jim said. "Perhaps they will listen to me now." He shook his

by Randolph Harris

hat-topped head and continued. "It's simply shameful that it takes scenes such as this to make one's voice heard."

The reporter moved the mobile microphone and Big Jim continued his grandstand rhetoric as he shook uninvited hands on his way to his chauffeur-driven car.

Later that evening in the 808 Club Dumont was sitting on a bar stool facing Monk. "Well, it happened just like you said it would. Everyone thinks that it was done by a rival street gang."

"Yeah, it was too bad about that broad and her child, but that's the way the cookie crumbles sometimes."

"Say, Monk, how about the payoff for those eastern guys?"

"Aw, I took care of that before I left the house. I called New York and had Bonito send someone by their place to pay them the balance."

"But I thought you didn't want Bonito to know about our business back here."

"That's right. That's why I told him the money was for a future job that those guys were going to do for me."

Beany was entering the tavern door. "Whatta you know?" he uttered, as he topped the stool, putting Monk in the middle.

"Hi," Monk greeted.

THE BLACK CONNECTION

"Hi, brother Beans," Dumont said, smiling. "Everything mellow? How's the new car running?"

"Man, it's beautiful!" And turning his head toward Monk, Beany said, "Thanks, Oscar."

Monk waved him away with his hand.

"Say, man," Dumont asked. "Did you see Alderman Sanders on TV? He really made a rousing speech, didn't he?"

"Yes, he did," Monk answered, "but don't pay any attention to that shit. That son-of-a-bitch will take a red-hot stove if you give it to him."

"Do you really think he's on the take?" Dumont asked.

"You hear that, Beany?" Monk twisted and looked at Beany, who was smiling. "I told you, Charlie. We run our thing just like the white boys do. Ole Big Jim has been on our payroll for two years now!"

"Ain't that a bitch?" Dumont said. "If you had heard that old bastard talk on TV, you'd have thought he was a damn minister."

"Shit, Charlie," Monk said. "That's politics. Big Jim is the cause of us having a Black police commander in this district. Didn't you know that Captain Peterson is Big Jim's man?"

"Hell, naw. It looks like I don't know nothing."

Monk got up from the stool and gave Dumont a friendly shoulder pat. "Don't worry, Charlie.

by Randolph Harris

You'll dig it all before long. I've got to make a call." Monk looked at his watch as he moved toward the wall phone.

Monk's conversation over the phone was quite brief. He cradled the receiver and returned to his bar stool. "Come on, you guys. Let's go upstairs."

The three men left the bar and entered the wooden door which led to the clubroom above. All were now settled in the room when Monk spoke. "I think it's safe to say that that bombing incident won't interfere with our personal business since everyone is blaming the street gangs."

Monk, casually and conservatively dressed as usual, leaned on his favorite dresser. "Now, as you two dudes know, we've got the best damn connection in the Midwest and I don't intend to blow it. Everyone will get their regular assignments; that is, excepting you, Charlie. You'll take over Red's operation, which is the street and bag business. And Charlie," Monk pointed out, "whenever one of those street dealers starts asking for stuff by the ounce, I want to know about it."

"I dig where you're coming from, man," Dumont announced.

"You see," Monk continued, "there's always some aggressive dudes around, and they might become valuable to our thing."

"Crazy," Dumont responded.

"Charlie," Monk went on to say, "since you haven't been on the scene too long, there are a few new guys you may not know. When that happens, I'm sure you know how to call some of us and check him out."

"No doubt about it," Dumont answered.

"A few of those westside guys have been coming over here copping. But, it's been proven that some of those motherfuckers just don't have any class."

"I know what'cha mean, man," Dumont answered.

Beany silently looked and listened.

"We're giving Big Jim enough bread to make sure that we're safe as long as we stay in Captain Peterson's district, but watch out for those damn Feds."

"I hear," Beany chimed in, "that some of those state guys have been fucking around out here on the south side."

"Well," Monk pointed out, "if we let any of them bust us, it's our own fault. Everybody knows not to do business with a stranger."

"Really!" Dumont butted in.

"Now, we've got dudes coming in from all parts of the country," Monk said, "and that's because we keep good dope. We've got a chance to lock this Midwest up. The older guys in the big white families have moved on to bigger and more legit things.

by Randolph Harris

And the Spics and Mexicans are satisfied with their wholesaling action. That leaves the field to us niggers to fight over and get rich."

"Man, I like that last part," Dumont remarked.

A knock came at the door. Beany opened it. "Hi, Tommy," he said.

"Brothers!" Tommy, a light, brown-skinned man, headed for the couch. "I figured you dudes were up here when I saw the cars downstairs. I dig that new wheel, Beany."

"Thanks." Beany was scratching for a cigarette.

Within the following hour, the room became full and, indeed, the agenda was quite illicit.

When Charlie Dumont proceeded from the old apartment and headed for his car, it had become dark. He switched on the headlights of the dark green sedan and steered the small car south. The car rolled along Cottage Grove Avenue, and eventually stopped in front of the huge apartment building. Dumont glanced at his watch and figured his mother would have dinner on the table. His eyes were attracted by two teenage lads who were coming out of Washington Park. Charlie's mind went to Jimmy, his younger brother. Wondering if Jimmy was home from the gym, Dumont entered the building and took the elevator up.

"Hi, Sugar." Charlie kissed his mother, a mingling grey-haired woman, then freed himself of

THE BLACK CONNECTION

his sport jacket. Mr. Dumont, Charlie's father, had died when Charlie was 12 years old. "Where's Jimmy?" he asked.

"Oh, he and that little boy named Sammy left together. They've been gone quite a while." Mrs. Dumont was strolling into the kitchen.

Charlie turned the faucet of the face bowl and began to hum. He had whiffed the aroma from the kitchen, and readjusting himself to homecooked food was indeed a treat. When the doorbell rang Dumont realized that Jimmy had a key. But where was he?

It was Mr. Steinberg, the janitor, telling Mrs. Dumont that both the washing machines in the laundry room were now repaired. Between bites, Dumont prodded his mother. "Where did they say there were going?"

Showing apprehensive signs, Mrs. Dumont placed a hand on her cheek and supported the other with her hip. "I've been wondering. He's never been this late." Then she left the kitchen.

When she walked away, Charlie sensed that his mother was going to peer from the front room window. The door rattled. Dumont turned his head. It was Jimmy.

Mrs. Dumont, dark-complexioned, stout and bosomy, was the first to speak. "Where have you been, boy?" Hands on her matured hips, she was

by Randolph Harris

not in the tiny hallway.

"Aw, Sammy and I were just out." Jimmy never stopped walking. He headed to the bathroom.

Dumont, completely stuffed but wanting to chat, called out. "Better come on before I eat up everything, man."

Coming out of the bathroom, Jimmy said, "Ain't hungry. Don't wanta eat." Then he continued to his room.

Mrs. Dumont, with an empty plate in her hand, looked at Charlie, her oldest son, who in turn stared back. She placed the clean plate on the table and proceeded to her baby son's room. Jimmy was lying across the bed.

"What's wrong? Didn't you go to the gym?"

"No, ma'am. We just fooled around." Jimmy never looked at his mother.

Claire Dumont momentarily stared at her son, then slowly backed out of the room.

"What's wrong with Jim?" Charlie inquired of his mother.

"I don't know. It's not like him. Why, he didn't even eat his dinner."

Dumont raised himself and urgently left the table.

"Come on, man. I know you're not that tired. Mama said that you and Sammy didn't go to the gym. What's wrong?"

THE BLACK CONNECTION

Jimmy rolled over and casually looked up at his big brother. He smiled. "Hi, Charlie. I guess I'm just tired. Sammy and I walked from the pool hall to home."

"That's more like it. How's the boxing coming along?"

"Aw, it's okay, but I haven't been to the gym in a couple days."

"You gotta watch that. In order to be a champ you gotta train." Dumont shook his kid brother by his head, then raised himself and left.

In the kitchen, Dumont said to his mother, "He's okay. He and Sammy were probably chasing each other across the park."

Dumont had fallen asleep on the front room couch.

The phone rang. "Hello ... Yeah, Tommy, what's happening? ... Where's Monk? ... Okay, pick me up in twenty minutes."

Reluctantly, Dumont raised himself from the couch and headed to the bathroom. When Tommy rolled up in the small blue Ford, Dumont was waiting at the curb. After the Ford turned at 60th Street, it headed east toward Stony Island Avenue. "Okay, Tommy, where is Monk and why all the rush, man?"

"I had to wait and tell you. You know what Monk said about talking over the telephone."

by Randolph Harris

"Yeah, yeah." Dumont nodded sarcastically.

"First of all, we're dirty." Tommy, an amiable-faced man, shot a furtive glance at Dumont, then stared straight ahead. "And second, we're on our way to Gary to make a delivery."

"Everything's cool. Just don't pick up no tickets. They might decide to search our ride."

Tommy turned the blue Ford carefully at Stony Island. A few blocks later, it was seen going up the Calumet Expressway ramp.

"Damn it," Tommy said. "That's why I like daytime driving. At least you can tell if you're being tailed."

"Just drive within the speed limits and let me worry about the rest." Charlie Dumont reached to his belt and removed the ominous-looking magnum. He broke the barrel and checked its full chambers, then replaced it snugly in his belt. "How much stuff have we got, and whereabouts in Gary are we taking it?"

"Monk told me to take a kilo to Morris' place. He said that you would know where it's at. Weren't you and him out there the other night?"

"Yeah," Dumont nodded. "Who're we supposed to see, and what about the bread?"

"Monk just told me to give it to Morris. I guess this is a consignment deal."

"Hum . . . Yeah, Monk's smart. He's doing it this

way to avoid a heist. He knows that those cold-blooded motherfuckers in Gary would kill their mammies for a load like this! I guess he'll have Morris bring the money to Chicago. That way, there can be no shit."

"I guess you're right."

The blue Ford rolled steadily along the expressway. Though not in the least was Tommy nervous, his dark eyes were constantly on the rear view mirror. Darkness shrouded the busy expressway while glaring beams haunted the concrete artery. Objects on the by-passed embankments loomed in assorted disfigurations, as the small Ford gobbled up the highway.

"You turn here, don't you?"

"Naw, Charlie. You've been away too long. That goes to west Gary. There's another exit further up the road."

"By the way," Charlie said, "you've never told me; just where is Monk?"

"Aw, he's shacked up with Dolly ... You know what?"

"What?"

"I think old Monk goes for that broad."

"There's no doubt about that. Who do you think pays for that apartment and those tough clothes she wears? That's why us dudes take these penitentiary chances; so we can get the things we

by Randolph Harris

like. Shit, Monk just likes a lot of broads. I don't blame him—I like 'em too."

"And me three," Tommy responded.

In the distance to the right the sky suddenly was aglow. Flames belched from the mouth of a red brick chimney as darkness devoured the tiny sparks. Similar structures displaying gusts of smoke were enmassed by gigantic industrial beams: the Midwestern city of steel—Gary.

"You know, we've got to be careful and watch our moves. There are some dangerous niggers over here."

"Now look, man. You don't have to tell me that." Tommy appeared insulted.

The car proceeded from the expressway lanes and very shortly halted at the toll gate. A kilo of undiluted heroin was in the car trunk. Casually, Tommy paid the toll guard and continued with his deadly load of contraband.

The street lights glared forlornly along Broadway Avenue as waxing treads of car tires echoed above the night. Dimly lit storefronts displayed mediocre fashions, while others showed scantily clad mannequins which were strongly protected by iron bars.

As the Illinois car approached 18th Street, a number of stores were boarded up. The car turned at 19th Street. It stopped. Its two occupants got

THE BLACK CONNECTION

out and entered the street level entrance.

Charlie Dumont didn't seem surprised that the atmosphere hadn't changed since he and Monk were last here. Females of mixed hues highlighted stools along the bar as fellows with long hair and fashionable dress whispered in their ladies' decorated ears. Dumont and Tommy continued to the rear and knocked at the door. It read PRIVATE. Very shortly, Dumont and Tommy returned to the trunk of the small blue Ford. But not until three young Black men took selected positions in V-shaped fashion on the corner of 19th Street.

To one not fully aware, it might have appeared quite strange that all three men had bulges on their sides. After removing a small brown shopping bag, Tommy slammed the car trunk shut, returned to the lively structure, walked past the bar and into the rear private enclosure. Dumont followed.

In less than five minutes the dope dealers had returned to their waiting car. When Tommy drove off, the three young Black men outside were still steadfast in their boomerang positions.

A fabulous bar and eatery had recently opened on 82nd and Cottage Grove Avenue. Its owner was a well known south side gambler who was reported to have connections that could easily weave a political path to the state capitol. In the upstairs dining room there were nothing but preferred

by Randolph Harris

guests, one of which was Alderman Harry Sanders who was facing Police Captain LaVerne Peterson, the present Commanding Officer of the gigantic Fifth District. Predominately Black, the district had often been appraised as the largest in the world, barring one in London.

Peterson, a large, brown-complexioned man, spoke. "Listen, Big Jim, you can tell those gullible reporters anything you want to, but you know that I don't buy that street gang bullshit! I'm the one who pulls your coat to the happenings out here, remember me?"

"Yeah, I know, Peterson, but I just don't want you to get carried away over this thing. Our bread and butter comes from the same places, you know?"

"I realize that, and I don't mind the gambling, the numbers, the policy, or even those damn whores' nests. But that fucking dope creates chaos and murder anywhere it settles."

"Now you listen to me, and maybe you'll remember who got you where you're at." Big Jim's face waxed as he bit down on his cigar.

"You're worried about the top brass downtown. Well, how do you think they sent their kids to school and bought those fine homes? Shit, I'd like to look inside some of their safe deposit boxes! Why, man, your district has been the reward to so

THE BLACK CONNECTION

many white commanders that I can't count 'em."

"That's just it," Peterson answered with displeasure. "They were white and didn't give a damn. But I'm Black and have three children out there in that cesspool. I go to bed every night thinking and wondering if that damn poison will eventually reach one of 'em."

"Well, you'd better start thinking of something else. There're three men on the waiting list who'd give their right arms to be in your position!"

The waitress brought two glasses of water and handed each man a menu.

chapter 5

MONK WAS TALKING TO SONYA as they sat at the breakfast table. "If the stuff continues to move as fast as it has been, we'll have to make another trip soon."

"I called Mr. Conway, the real estate man. He told me about a beautiful home that's up for sale, out in the Pill Hill district. You remember, you promised that we would buy a home after that last pick up."

"If it's what you think you want, buy it. In case I have to take another fall, at least I'll have a home to return to."

Monk's handsome dark features showed little concern. His interest was devoted to his morning paper. A small paragraph in the second column caught his eye. His broad nose flared; his strong cheek-bones twitched nervously. He was unaware that he was gritting his pearly teeth.

Familiar with Monk's silent anger, Sonya asked, "What's wrong?"

THE BLACK CONNECTION

"They've let those motherfuckers out!"

"Who?"

"That little bitch who killed Red. Her and that dope fiend. They're both out!"

"What're you going to do?"

"What do you think?"

Angrily, Monk balled up his napkin, flung it to the table and raised himself. He grabbed the phone and began to dial. Sonya was entering the kitchen and the last thing she heard Monk say was, "Make sure that they don't have that baby with them!"

Sonya flinched.

Sonya had been married to Oscar (Monk) Davis for five years. Formerly an expensive call girl, Sonya had met Monk while devotedly plying her trade. Attracted by each other's pragmatic ambitions to conquer the pitfalls of ghetto life, they were ritually united. And of course, the instilled longing for motherhood, plus a dogmatic vow to attain a tranquil life had hardened her morally. Three times aborted, Sonya, at age twenty-six, was determined to have kids. Sensing that the order for the two persons' deaths already had been issued, Sonya was overjoyed that the life of the infant would be spared.

"Do you still want me to place the mortgage in my father's name?"

"You're damn right I do! You know that I can't

by Randolph Harris

own anything in our name—not with my penitentiary record."

"Yeah, you filed a Pauper's Writ when you were released, didn't you?"

"You're fucking right I did! My fine was ten thousand dollars, plus I did three and a half years."

Sonya had dirty dishes in her hands as she responded. "Well, I really can't see us paying the government that ten thousand dollars. It will only cause the Internal Revenue to look further into our business."

"Damn right." Monk donned a canvas-colored pea-jacket, which didn't exactly match his beige-hued slacks. He kissed Sonya on the cheek and headed for the door. He turned. "If Charlie calls, I'll be at the bar."

"Okay," Sonya nodded.

Agents Danny Gruff and Sidney Miller were riding north along Lake Shore Drive. Their office headquarters was situated on LaSalle Street.

"I think the chief is trying to bring this case together before it becomes too wide-spread," Gruff remarked.

"Has a report come in on their Detroit activities, yet?" Miller turned to look at his partner as they passed moving cars.

"Yeah, I'm sure it has. That's probably the

reason for this grouping."

Miller steered the inconspicuous car left at Randolph Street. Even though it was slightly past midday, Randolph Street was as usual substantially lighted. The Oriental Theatre's giant marquee blinked as the flashing bulbs brought to mind the running of small mice. Its counterpart, the Woods, also toasted a stellar attraction as the human line which began at the Greyhound Bus Depot plainly foretold.

The agent's car halted for the red light at Clark Street. Entering their headquarters on LaSalle Street, the agents proceeded to the large assembling room. It consisted of sparsely pictured walls and chairs. A manicured group made up of ten individuals was already present. Some of their faces brought to mind recent college graduates. A couple could have been young lawyers glowing with future promise. And there were some, including the entering two, who dripped with clandestine never-you-mind. And yet, they were all agents of the Federal Narcotics Division.

Chicago Divisional Director Ralph E. Hines entered from another door. The murmurs ceased. There were sounds of folders closing. Disciplined attentiveness was shown to the tall grey-headed full-faced man.

Not bothering to sit, Director Hines' eyes

by Randolph Harris

beamed down the long, wide, varnished table. "Gentlemen, at our last briefing I explained how fast this Black outfit had been expanding. And after compiling data gathered from throughout," Director Hines leaned forward, "the reports substantiate the theory that there definitely is a 'Black Connection.'"

Tall, with a military walk, the chief agent pulled down a wall map that was on a roller. It hovered above a wide blackboard. "Our reports show that Jamaica is the distributing location for the narcotics that are destined for New York and Canadian seaports. And right here," Hines was using a ball-point pen as a pointer, "they follow this ocean path through Port au Prince and dock at Haiti. A boat then takes the contraband around Guantanamo Bay, the U.S. Naval Base, and then docks off the shores of Santiago Province."

The director turned from the map and faced his subordinates. "From this point, we haven't been able to learn their methods or means of transportation. Probably a hidden airport somewhere in the density of the mountainous province."

Chief Hines walked back to the head of the long table and continued. "We do know, however, that the same shipments that have previously left Jamaica eventually wound up in Canada. And there, it is received by a Mafia family controlled by

THE BLACK CONNECTION

Santino Serritelli; a Don who is based in New York.

"There have been speculations that the shipments arrive at New York ports, and from there it is filtered into Canada by way of Buffalo. However, this is just theory. We also know that the shipments have eventually wound up in the possession of this Chicago Black outfit. Therefore, gentlemen, from now until its completion, case number 10572 shall be known as the 'Black Connection.'"

Hines glanced at the round clock which had been neatly built within the wall. He continued. "Shortly, we shall be joined by two Eastern Divisional agents who have come here to give us a first hand account of the connection's procedural hookup. All indications, from their taped report which earlier preceded them, tends to show that this hookup occurs at the Windsor Racetrack in Windsor, Canada. A few steps out of Detroit, Michigan."

Chief Agent Hines bent to his vacant chair at the head of the table. "Now, I don't have to tell you that this heroin is of the highest quality. Our buyers and informers have made available to us samples of its outstanding purity."

The buzzer sounded from the only phone on the table. Hines extended a hand that boasted well-manicured fingernails and lifted it. "Yes ... Send

by Randolph Harris

them in." A slight pause and then two Black men entered from the outer office.

"Gentlemen," Director Hines said, "perhaps some of you have already met. These are Agents Roscoe E. Brown and Wesley Phillips."

Nods and bows from everyone. There also were a few smiling expressions, indicating signs of previous association.

Two vacant chairs awaiting occupancy were filled. Chief Hines, looking more the banker than a chief custodian, raised from his seat.

"In a moment, we shall hear Agents Brown and Phillips' first hand reports. But I want to impress upon you that we're through with the tactics of reconnaissance. From here on, we shall strive for infiltration, sale, and possession. And I'm expecting a signed document from the director in Washington which should give us the authority to go ahead with our electronic facilities. We must try to get evidence and apprehend any of the outfit's subordinates. Remember, like any other chain, there are always weak links in a connection."

Chief Hines settled in his seat. There began a rustling of folders. Snapping sounds from attache cases filled the room as reports were being spread.

The following morning, Charlie Dumont was sitting on the edge of his bed. His mother, Claire

THE BLACK CONNECTION

Dumont, said, "Are you going to have breakfast before you go?"

"Naw, Ma, I don't feel like eating just now." Charlie entered the bathroom.

Mrs. Dumont glanced out the window and across the street. In the park, a ballgame made up of neighborhood kids was about to shape up. She strained her eyes for Jimmy, then turned and looked at the clock. Eleven o'clock—Jimmy had been gone for well over an hour. Where was Sammy? Mrs. Dumont could see no trace of Jimmy's friend.

Charlie Dumont sauntered out of the bathroom. "Ma, I've got some business to take care of. I probably won't return until late tonight."

"Charles, I wish you'd get a decent job and leave those numbers alone. What if you're picked up? It'll be right back to that penitentiary for violating your parole."

Charles Dumont had told his mother that he was picking up numbers for a neighborhood numbers banker.

"Now, Ma, don't worry your pretty head about me. I told you that Mr. Whitfield, the parole officer, and I have an understanding. As long as I don't get into any serious trouble, he's promised me that he would square it. And, anyway, where could I find a job with my record that would pay me as

by Randolph Harris

much money? I only work about two hours a day picking up numbers slips. And if any of the players hit, I get ten percent of what they win. You can't beat that."

"Well, I guess I just worry too much."

Mrs. Dumont sat on the living room couch, and her son continued on to his room to dress.

"You know, Charles, it hasn't been easy for me since your father died. After you were grown, my mind became a bit more settled. Then you got that job at the wholesale house and I figured between the two of us, we might've been able to send Jimmy to college. But when you went and got into that trouble, I worried a lot about you. And quite naturally, I began to worry more about Jimmy's future." Mrs. Dumont had unfolded the morning paper.

Dumont stepped from his room. He was buttoning his shirt. "Look, like you said, I'm grown now, and, believe me, Ma, you don't have to worry about me. As for Jimmy, I'm going to see to it that he goes to college." Dumont adjusted his shirt within his pants.

"Lord! This city is getting awful." Claire Dumont was straining her eyes at the newspaper.

"What happened now?" Charlie reentered the room.

"It says here that they found a woman and her

THE BLACK CONNECTION

husband dead in an apartment down on 50th Street. They'd both been shot twice in the head."

"Probably a robbery." Dumont had on his leather sports jacket. He was preparing to leave.

"I don't know about that. It says here that they were both released on bond and were scheduled to appear in court on a murder charge later this month."

Charlie Dumont hesitated, twisted his head. "What were their names?"

"Let's see... Yeah, here it is. Miss Sylvia Jones and Robert Smith. It says that the landlady had rented them the apartment as man and wife. It seems that somebody heard the baby crying and went in to investigate. Both bodies had been bound and gagged."

"Let's see that." Charlie bent over his mother's shoulder and peered at the newspaper. He straightened. "Like I said, probably a case of robbery." Dumont kissed his mother on the cheek and headed for the door. "By the way, what time did Jimmy leave this morning?"

"Aw, he and Sammy went over to the park about ten o'clock." Mrs. Dumont raised herself from the couch and stepped over to the window.

"Has he been going to the gym?"

"I don't think so," Mrs. Dumont answered. "I heard them mention the pool hall a few times

by Randolph Harris

lately. I'll be glad when school starts again."

"The pool hall? On my way, I'll walk over to the park and see if I can spot them." Dumont went out the door.

Later that evening, Dumont and Monk were leaving the cab stand around the corner on Vincennes Avenue.

"How did you come out?"

Monk was counting his money. "I may have lost a few dollars. I walked around there trying to catch a dude who owed me some bread and the fellas just happened to be shooting dice."

"I saw the papers this morning. I guess that squares things for Red."

"It was something that had to be done."

Monk and Dumont continued along 47th Street. Monk, tall and swaggering, Dumont, short and quick-stepping.

At 5 P.M. that same evening Tommy picked Dumont up at the 808 Club. The blue Ford took both men to Monk's house. Sonya opened the door.

"Hi, Charlie. Oscar called and said that you and Tommy would be by. Got to make a meet, huh?"

"Hi, Sonya. Yeah, I left Tommy in the car. I told him to pick me up around back."

"You told him right. You never know who's watching. Come on downstairs."

THE BLACK CONNECTION

Sonya carefully locked her first floor apartment door and proceeded to the basement. Dumont followed. She selected a key from her key ring and entered. Sonya pressed a wall button and immediately light flooded the crypt-like structure.

The concrete floor crunched grittily beneath their feet as they treaded past a row of washing machines and dryers.

"Hold it." Sonya stopped and pressed another wall button, used another key, then they both walked through the brown-panelled door.

The basement enclosure contained metal lockers similar to those in a gymnasium. Each locker had a metal plate on which was engraved an apartment number. Bold security locks hung heavily from all of them.

Sonya traveled to one of the metal booths and began to dial a huge combination lock. Charlie was quick to note that this particular locker had no apartment number plate whatsoever. After pawing under bundles of seemingly discarded clothes, Sonya produced a plastic bag in which glowed a white powdery substance. She held out the plastic package to Dumont. "Here, wait a minute. Better put it in this."

"Yeah, this is mellow." Dumont placed the plastic package inside the paper bag and folded it. Sonya closed the locker.

by Randolph Harris

"You know Monk and I are buying a home out south. I'll be glad to leave this neighborhood."

"I know what'cha mean, Sonya."

Dumont then left the rear entrance of the building. Tommy was patiently awaiting him with the car motor running. It was 5:38 P.M. when the blue Ford rolled out of the alley and headed west toward the Dan Ryan Expressway. Just before Tommy turned the corner at the end of the block—always on the alert for a tail—he thought he saw a black car come out of the alley and turn in his direction. He speeded the blue Ford and turned left on St. Lawrence Avenue. The Ford was only midway down the block when Tommy looked into the rear view mirror and saw that the mysterious black car also had turned the corner. Coincidence? He didn't think so. He gunned the car and turned right at 49th Street. No doubt about, the black car had turned also.

"We've got a tail!" Tommy said excitedly.

Dumont turned and looked past the wide rear window, answering Tommy in the same movement. "Hit it, man! Hit it!"

The small blue car was traveling like a jet. Disregarding the red lights, swerving and forcing other cars to apply their brakes, the blue Ford thundered across King Drive. The ominous black car containing two white occupants was gaining.

THE BLACK CONNECTION

Tommy miraculously steered the car across State Street and was going through the underpass. Dumont yelled, "Take the expressway! Take the expressway!"

With a sudden move, Tommy turned the screeching wheels left. Now the small blue car was speeding down the expressway ramp.

"Wait! Wait!" Dumont's face was distorted with anguish. It was too late. Tommy had taken the wrong turn! He was FACING traffic!

Dumont through of the hot, confining penitentiary cell. His kid brother Jimmy's image materialized as did all things in those computerized seconds.

Tommy, unquestionably, was a master at the wheel as the on-coming drivers could surely, though frightfully, testify. A large transport truck was in the far right lane. The blue Ford had just swerved from the center lane in order to avoid an oncoming green sedan. Dumont braced himself for the inevitable crash. Tommy applied the brakes. The small blue car slid, burnt rubber, and spun. It was now headed in the opposite direction! The truck had braked and swerved into the next lane, thus missing the green sedan.

The chasing black car contained two befuddled white men as Tommy could clearly see when he rocketed past them. The grey-haired man was lean-

by Randolph Harris

ing out the window on the passenger's side. A threatening gun was in his hand.

Dumont, realizing that the men were obviously hesitant to shoot because of the heavy flowing traffic, reached to his inside pocket and produced a knife. Tommy, slightly more composed, glanced at the rear view mirror. "They've straightened out, and here they come again!"

"Yeah." Sensing he had made a bad suggestion, Dumont said, "And they've probably dispatched cars to block the exit ramps. Just keep driving. They won't shoot." Charlie took his knife and savagely ripped the plastic package. He gripped the bag firmly with both hands, then held the package outside the open window.

The terrific speed against the wind caused the plastic bag to ripple. Blowing powder resembling snow polluting the mild evening breeze. Drivers passing by stared in amazement and instantly reckoned it as some childish prank. Tommy yelled, "They're closing in on us!" Dumont dusted himself and reached for his cigarette lighter.

"Okay, Tommy, pull over and keep cool."

Tommy steered the car over on the grassy embankment. He and Dumont sat with their hands clearly raised.

Agents Danny Gruff and Sidney Miller advanced on the small blue Ford with pistols drawn. Agent

THE BLACK CONNECTION

Gruff stood at the rear left of the car, and Agent Miller stood at the right. "Get out of the car with your hands behind your heads!" Gruff commanded.

After both men had leaned on the car, they were thoroughly searched and then handcuffed. Gruff proceeded to search the car, which had previously carried deadly drugs. His nose detected a pungent odor.

"Hey, Sid, come over here."

Agent Miller moved toward the front seat of the small Ford, keeping well-trained eyes on his two handcuffed prisoners.

"Do you get that smell?"

"Yeah," Miller grunted. "Plastic."

"The bastards burnt the bag. Look!" Gruff was leaning down into the car. His fingers rubbed the floor mat. He straightened and continued to rub his thumb against his fingers. "Ashes."

"Yeah," Miller muttered.

chapter 6

TWO WEEKS LATER, Agents Gruff and Sidney Miller were riding along Lake Shore Drive. They had just completed a successful meeting in which they collaborated their reports with those of two Eastern Divisional Agents and the one from Interpol.

"Sid, sometimes this fucking job stinks. We spot two creeps making with a package, and figured it to be a bag of misery. We chase the sons-of-bitches, and what happens? They throw the shit in our faces!"

"Yeah, Danny, I know."

"But it gets my Irish up when I realize there's not a damn thing we can do about it. A measly reckless driving charge. You'd have thought the judge was one of their family. What do you think about the trend the country is in, Sid?"

"Well, Danny, I'll tell you. Nine guys with black robes tell us which way we should think."

"Yeah, yeah, I know. They make the laws and

THE BLACK CONNECTION

we enforce them, but I wish they'd get around to my way of thinking."

The car passed Buckingham Fountain and used the green water of Lake Michigan for background.

"What do you think of that rumble out of Haiti?" Miller looked straight ahead.

"When those Interpol jockeys say they've heard noise of a large shipment, you can bet your shirt it's a big one." Danny was blunt.

"All liaisons seem to think that the shipment has already left Haiti."

Both men were hatless as Agent Gruff ran his fingers through his grey mane. "As yet, Interpol hasn't been able to locate the airport. But they figure it's somewhere in Santiago Province," Dan said.

"That means the next time we hear of the stuff it'll be inside the States!"

"And our job will be to intercept it in Canada."

"That's what the chief said."

The agents' car bearing Tennessee license plates turned from Lake Shore Drive and cruised west on 47th Street.

"What are the lines on this Don, Santino Serritelli?" Miller asked.

"I remember a few years back when a Senate subcommittee subpoenaed him. I was on the Hertzfeld case during that period, but I remember he

by Randolph Harris

took the 'Fifth' forty-five times. Nothing ever came out of the case."

"One of those honorable men, huh?"

"Yeah, it took a biggie like him to set up a snake-back operation like this."

"An astute guy?"

"Very. You know what, Sid? With a large operation like this, there has got to be records someplace."

The agents parked on 47th Street near the 808 Club. About the same time Tommy was coming out the entrance of an apartment building on Forrestville Avenue. He was scheduled to meet an old customer whose drug operations were in Minnesota. He had no idea that tragedy was about to strike.

Tommy paid small heed to the green station wagon parked at the curb. It was indeed ironic that the man who was forever suspecting a tail never saw the three youths who swiftly came up behind him. And, of course, when he heard them, it was too late. A karate neck chop put Tommy out of his consciousness and the murderously wielded knives put him out of this world.

Leaving Tommy's punctured and lifeless body lying on the blood-soaked car seat, three Afro-haired youths walked calmly to the green station wagon. As the old vehicle roared away, it was quite

THE BLACK CONNECTION

obvious that all three youths had earlier agreed that it was just something that had to be done.

Dolly, Monk, Dumont, Beany, and George, a comely, medium-built man, were all scattered along the 808 Club bar. The gathering had turned into quite a hilarious celebration.

Monk, with an arm around Dolly's waist, turned to Dumont, who was mounted on the next stool. "Damn it, Charlie, I would like to have seen the looks on those coppers' faces after you had destroyed all the incriminating evidence!"

"I'm sorry that I had to throw away that half a kilo, Monk. But I know you dig why."

"You're damn right," Monk answered. "It would have been all right if it had been a whole kee. But, tell me, man, how did the fuzz get a line on you and Tommy?"

"I've been thinking about that," Dumont answered. "They must have been cruising and just happened to spot me with that package as I came out to the alley."

"With Tommy parked and waiting for you, it might have looked suspicious to them," Monk indicated. "By the way," he said, looking around, "where is Tommy?"

"I talked to him after we left the court room. He told me that he had a meet with a guy from

by Randolph Harris

Minnesota tonight," Dumont answered.

Monk gently pushed Dolly away and reached to his pocket for his cigarettes. "Yeah, that would be ole Treetops. He and his woman generally drive in and cop a kee. Tommy will probably be through here after he makes the pitch. Do you think that those guys who busted you could have been Feds?"

Dumont sat his drink down and swallowed. "I don't think so," he answered. "They called in over their dispatch phone, and pretty soon a police van picked us up and took Tommy and me to the lock-up. Then, after we made bond, Alderman Sanders told us what lawyer to get. When we finally went back to court, the lawyer told us to plead guilty to reckless driving and pay the fine. The dudes who busted us wasn't even there. I haven't seen them since."

"Remember," Monk asked, "when Beany spoke of those State guys who were snooping around out here?"

"Hey, Beany." Monk flicked his hand and crooked his finger.

Beany traveled the length of the bar and stopped in front of Monk. "What's happening?"

"Who was it," Monk asked, "that told you about those State men?"

Beany gently stroked his processed hair and

answered. "Aw, that was Poindexter . . ."

"You mean Detective Poindexter, the policeman?" Dumont interrupted.

"Yeah," Beany answered. "Tell him, Monk."

"He's okay," Monk pointed out. "Big Jim helped to get him out of that blue uniform, so Poindexter, anxious to climb the ladder fast, goes along with the show. He delivers news that he picks up at the District. He's in the book. Which reminds me. That's all, Beany." Monk turned back to Dumont after Beany had walked away.

"I've got some books—records and all that shit—that I want you to keep for a while." Monk glanced toward Dolly, who was playing the vendor. He added, "Sonya and I will be packing to move pretty soon, and I don't want to misplace the books during the hassle. I used to keep them in a safety deposit box. But it was too much trouble going back and forth when I needed them. Our thing has gotten so big that I make entries every day."

Dumont answered through a puff of smoke. "You know I'll keep 'em man. Nobody at the house but Mom and Jimmy. You can bet they'll be safe there. That reminds me, Jimmy goes back to school next week."

The ring of the wall phone conquered the sounds from the blatant juke box. George called

by Randolph Harris

Monk, while holding the receiver. "Sounds like it's Sonya."

Dolly, who was talking to a newly-arrived girl friend, allowed her eyes to follow Monk as he grasped the receiver from George.

"Hello..." A few minutes passed and Monk replaced the receiver. Curiously, he sauntered back to his stool.

"Is everything cool?" asked Dumont.

Monk, brandishing a look that moved past the man in front of him, said, "That was Sonya. She said that someone just found Tommy's body in his car. He'd been stabbed fifteen or twenty times. His body was taken to the morgue."

With ostensible shock, Charlie said, "But... who?..."

"You know fucking well who did it. Those motherfucking 'Angels.' They call themselves getting even for that bombing—the bastards!"

"You mean that street gang?"

"Damn it, Charlie, who else?"

The hot September day was surely out of line with the axis as summer stubbornly accepted the challenge of fall. Stumbling tots carrying dangling school books cluttered the sidewalks. It could be called a day of Indian summer.

Dumont was driving Monk's dark gray Olds-

THE BLACK CONNECTION

mobile and Monk was sitting beside him.

"Sonya told me you picked up the books yesterday."

"Yeah, I did. Well, Monk, what about Tommy?"

"Man, you know I'm going to take care of it."

"Yeah."

"But there's something big about to jump off. I got a call from Bonito last night. And from what he tells me, this load could make us rich."

"Any catches?"

"The usual. Money."

"How much have you got to come up with?"

"A half million."

Charlie Dumont whistled. "Some catch."

"Aw, that won't be a problem. But it will take all our bread, plus the balance of our stuff. Remind me to call Morris; he'll probably take a kee at a hurry-up price. The rest we can dump up in Wisconsin."

"When you say big, you're not kidding, are you?"

"Charlie, you've been out here long enough to see what's happening. The only things that whiteys respect are money and power. And, daddy, when you've got money, you have them both. Just to show you, the other day Sonya went to see about our new house out in Pill Hill. Ole man Conway, the real estate dealer, had asked a price of sixty

by Randolph Harris

thousand dollars. I paid one of the office girls to find out for me who the owner was. By having cash money, I was able to give Sonya's father twenty thousand; the owner held the paper and I saved ten thousand dollars."

"Damn, that was a lot of extra bread. Why was Conway trying to rip you off for so much?" Dumont stopped for the red light at 43rd Street.

"Shit, Charlie, that's the *Black* price. If a Black wants to live decently, he's got to pay a bigger price. That's why we've got to get big scratch, man."

"So this is the big one, huh?"

"Yeah," Monk answered, pawing for a cigarette. "When we make this trip, we'll clear close to two million dollars. The stuff will reach Canada in two weeks, according to Bonito."

Charlie bent the corner at Oakwood Boulevard. "Didn't you say we were going to check on those cutters?"

"Yeah," Monk answered. "Then we can compare and tell how much stuff we have on hand. Remind me to call Sonya so she can stop at Sol's Restaurant and pick up six dinners for them."

"How long have they been working?"

Monk glanced at his only valued piece of jewelry and answered. "Sonya told me that she locked them in about 9 o'clock this morning."

THE BLACK CONNECTION

"You're sure they have no way to slip anything out?"

"Hell, no. The only ventilation is the air-conditioner, and the window is nailed down tight against it. It's Sonya's job to see that they get what they need, which is nothing but cigarettes and food. And there's a convenient phone if it becomes necessary."

"I guess you're right. They'd steal you blind if you didn't lock 'em in. What about searching them when they're through cutting the stuff?"

"That's my job. But now that you're back," he looked at Dumont and smiled, "we're going to share that burden. You see, Charlie, outside of Sonya, you're the only one I can really trust."

"Thanks, Monk. You'll never be sorry."

The car continued along Oakwood Boulevard and slowed as it approached the alley at Forrestville Avenue. Dumont pulled up in a vacant lot. Both men alighted and walked through a gangway which brought them out on Evans Avenue. The entire neighborhood was a complete eyesore. Rundown apartment buildings jammed together like cans of salmon.

The two dope dealers entered a rubbish-littered yard and proceeded up a flight of worn-out stairs at the rear of a red brick building, came to the second floor, and stopped. Dumont noticed the

by Randolph Harris

two boarded-up windows as Monk produced a key and gained entrance.

The were six young Black men present; three on each side of a long wooden table. All of them wore surgical masks. The potent fumes from the high grade heroin obviously made the masks a necessity. Dumont glanced about the large room. Light was provided by a high-powered bulb dangling from the ceiling at the end of an electric cord. Excepting the protruding air-conditioner and the chairs occupied by the six men, the dingy abode was bare. There was a small toilet off to the right. This consisted of a face bowl and commode.

Monk spoke. "How's it going, fellas?"

Positive comments came from assorted voices. At one end of the long table were varying sizes of plastic packages; white powder loomed from within each of them. At the other end was a large sifter next to stacked empty bags and a small portable scale so intricately mantled that a feather would disturb its weighing fractions. On the floor sat a five gallon tin container which was partially filled with harmless milk sugar. This was used to dilute the potent heroin.

Monk began counting the sealed plastic bags. "Like I told you, Charlie, we're in good shape," Monk said, fingering a pound bag of the deadly drugs. "With these and the other bags, we should

THE BLACK CONNECTION

make our quota in a week or ten days." Monk replaced the package atop the table and continued to inspect the remains of them.

Unknown to Monk and the other occupants in the house, furtive reconnaissance was going on outside. A shabby green station wagon made waxing, crunching sounds as its tires rolled slowly through the garbage-littered alley.

The station wagon slowed as it passed Monk's dark grey Oldsmobile. Two Afro-headed youths were sitting in the front. A third porcupine-headed lad raised from the rear of the vehicle and jotted down the license number of the Oldsmobile.

Continuing, the green station wagon left the mouth of the alley and parked on Oakwood Boulevard. Street lights had made their first glow as Monk and Charlie Dumont descended the rear stairs. Dumont slid under the wheel as Monk casually plopped beside him. Dumont steered the car south.

Forty-seventh Street boasted its usually busy activities. Drug inhabited bodies sauntered back and forth across the street. Neon signs twisted to shape the images of hot dogs and chickens repeatedly blinked off and on. Juke boxes blasted with the latest rhythmic beats as Dumont braked the car in front of the 808 Club.

A moment later, a dark green station wagon was

by Randolph Harris

seen slowly turning the corner. Inside the tavern, Oscar (Monk) Davis, muscular and tall, and Charlie Dumont, mildly short and trim, reassembled the large and small of things.

Dolly, small and petite, a slightly opposite figure from Monk's wife, sat glowingly as the two dope dealers entered the bar.

Beany, with toast brown complexion and a glossy head of processed hair, leaned on the bar rapping to George, his round face smiling. George listened intently.

"I got bored waiting for you to call me," Dolly said to Monk, who had stopped in front of her. He leaned both elbows on the bar and twisted his head.

"Hey, Beany. How's the new car riding?"

"Peaches, man." Beany diverted his attention from George to Monk. "You haven't let me take you for a ride yet."

"I've got to take the car to Sonya in a few minutes. Maybe I'll let you drive me home. George or Charlie could follow us," Monk said, looking at his watch.

"Say, Oscar, isn't it about time for Sonya to make that run?" Charlie had thought about the dope cutters receiving their dinner.

"Yeah, that's right." Monk was gazing at his watch; then turning to Dolly, he spoke again. "I'll

THE BLACK CONNECTION

be by your apartment in an hour."

"What about those things I told you about?" Dolly asked, staring with small brown eyes.

"Don't worry about them," Monk answered. "I'll give you the bread tonight."

Oscar gingerly patted Dolly on her cheek, then turned. "Come on, Charlie. Let's go."

"Here, man," Beany said, throwing Monk the new car keys. "Take my car. George and me will follow you."

"Come on, Charlie," Oscar said. "Let's feel how a new car rides." All four men filed out onto the sidewalk.

"See you dudes at the house," Monk said, as he and Dumont strolled toward the shiny red sedan parked at the curb.

Bright lights illuminated 47th Street as Beany steered the grey Olds through perpetual traffic. Unknown to him or his calm companion George, was the dark green station wagon which stalked Beany's every turn. Beany steered left at Vincennes Avenue and the grey Oldsmobile rolled past the old folks' home which was situated to the right. Its dimly lighted windows glowed serenely as the green station wagon also passed it by.

Beany was driving through Washington Park. "I forgot that Monk moved farther out south."

"Yeah," George answered. "He and Sonya

by Randolph Harris

moved some things the other day."

The Olds was passing the Armory and the green station wagon was not far behind. Most abruptly, however, the green vehicle shot forward. It went around the Oldsmobile, positioning itself in front of the car. The station wagon suddenly slowed, and its rear windows were rolled down.

Anyone witnessing the two popped-up Afro heads unquestionably would have visualized "Jack-in-the-box." In unison, the two heads were gazing down long, twin double-barreled shotguns. The four simultaneous blasts echoed loudly above the night. The windshield of the Oldsmobile was completely disintegrated, and the last two shots were entirely unnecessary.

The dark grey Olds veered toward the park foliage as the green station wagon hastily put on speed. There was an explosive crash which produced crimson flames. Engulfed were the bodies of Beany and George.

The next morning in Monk's newly acquired home, Monk and Dumont sat in the breakfast nook.

"Well, Monk," Charlie said, "I guess you know they were after you and me?"

"I'd be a damn fool not to realize it. Damn it, Charlie, that's what I'm trying to make you fellas understand. Yes, you included. You see, Charlie, I

THE BLACK CONNECTION

understand these young dudes. They see guys like you and me handling money every day, and they realize we've got a damn good connection somewhere. Now they want in, but they're just too young to get in. Are you following me?"

Charlie replaced his cup of half-filled coffee and said, "Rap on. I'm digging you."

"Okay, now look at it this way." Monk secured his Japanese designed robe and continued. "If these dudes were old enough, I'd have them with us. But . . . " Monk raised one finger, "that doesn't mean that they don't know what's happening. Why, shit, man, to them there's a war going on right here in this country. A war that's designed to keep them, as Black people and all other minorities, at the bottom of the ladder. A lot of those young dudes have got brains, man. But they don't have any outlet to use them. In other words, we're the closest thing to them, so they use their brains on us. Shit, they don't give a damn if we're white or Black. To them, we provide a means of escape.

"See, Charlie, everything that they know they've learned from the whitey. They see the rich whiteys living off the poor whiteys. They've read about the old time Irish gangs that were here in Chicago years ago. They know about the Italians, how they brained each other, and how they, the Italians, whether it's acknowledged or not, have become a

by Randolph Harris

power structure to be reckoned with. So they, as Blacks, figure that it's only a way of life in this country that they should reach their destiny through the exploitation of their own. They don't give a damn about going to the joint, man. It's a well known fact that some of them actually live better in the joint. Pass me that sugar, Charlie."

Monk cut his coffee with two spoons and continued. "As they already know, some of them are going to be killed, but doesn't somebody in every war? Shit, eighty percent of their parents don't earn enough to pay the bills, much less support some teenage boys. And I'm damn sure that you realize there are not enough jobs for the poor whites."

"Damn, man," Charlie interrupted, "you act like you're defending the bastards who tried to off us!"

"Hell, no, I'm not defending the motherfuckers! But I am saying, I know how they feel. If my old man hadn't gotten himself croaked in that steel mill accident, my old lady wouldn't have had enough money for me to finish high school. You know my brother Louis died from pneumonia when he was only ten years old."

"You know I remember, man." Dumont blew cigarette smoke and it floated through the open nook windows. A mild September breeze parted the pink-flowered curtains.

THE BLACK CONNECTION

"And getting back to what I was saying," Monk dabbed his cigarette. "Like me, if some of them are lucky enough to even finish high school, because they're Black, they still won't receive a decent job.

"A year after I was out of high school, I was in the joint." Monk went on. "And it was all because I couldn't find a fucking job. So I began creeping—until one night the rollers busted me inside a crib over north. That's how I got a chance to meet Santino. An older guy named Guido, who had been a Capo in Santino's family back East, had taken a fall and the family couldn't square it. He pulled ten. I was doing three to five at the time."

"One night, before we went in for lock-up, I saved Guido from getting a shiv. We became friends; he even taught me a few words in Italian. When I came up for parole, Guido still had a few years to pull. However, he told me, if ever I was in New York City, I was to go by a certain restaurant and tell the owner that Guido sent me, and also tell him I wanted to get in touch with Santino Serritelli. Ever since then, things have been easy."

"What the hell," Dumont remarked. "They did you a favor when they sent you to the joint."

"No doubt about it," Monk responded. "And a lot of those young dudes know that the penitentiary is a mainstay when it comes to making connections. You know that from your own

by Randolph Harris

experience, Charlie."

"You're fucking right I do."

"Just look around and tell me, Charlie, where could I get a salary that would allow me to buy a home and live like this? Come on, I'm going to show you the place."

"Crazy." Dumont raised from his chair and followed Monk into an oversized dining room. The maid had just finished polishing the silverware and the eating utensils sparkled above carefully placed white napkins. Expensive high-backed chairs surrounded the large dining table, and the highly polished floors shone of a golden background.

Dumont followed Monk into the next lavishly furnished room. Clearly, it was fit for a king. Velvety papered walls held the room in captivity. All the assorted furnishings demonstrated elegant taste. The aqua-hued shag rug boasted a depth that resembled grass. Stairs that spiraled to three bedrooms above revealed architectural expertise. The first displayed a bed that appeared to sleep six, its design French Provincial with a subtle touch of white. Light blue carpet flooded every inch of the enclosure.

Dumont gazed through the bedroom window and focused on a widespread green lawn. "This is it, Monk! This is it!"

"You like, huh?"

THE BLACK CONNECTION

"You're damn right, I do."

"Come on," Monk said. "I'll show you the other bedrooms."

Dumont followed Monk into the thickly carpeted hallway. "Say, man. What are we gonna do about those Black Angels?"

"I'm going to put so much pressure on those motherfuckers, they won't know which way to turn! How do you like that?"

Monk had entered the second bedroom. He was showing Charlie the enormous heart-shaped bed. "Sonya had it especially made." Monk went on to say, "They put the last part together right here in the room. It was too large to bring inside otherwise."

"Yeah, I see what'cha mean. But Monk, we've got to be damn careful now that those young dudes know that they missed us."

"How do you like these drapes?" Monk was fingering the heavily-hung shantung green drapes.

"Yeah, they're boss. But man, we've got to get ourselves together. I go along with you about those dudes. They're playing for keeps." Dumont's face showed deep sincerity.

"Don't worry, man. Just don't worry." Monk had put a fatherly hand on Dumont's shoulder.

"Look, Monk, you know there is nothing chicken about me, but these little bastards have

by Randolph Harris

started coming out of the walls. You just don't know when or where they might pop up."

"Look, Charlie, we've been an easy target for those punks simply because they always knew where to find us. But you can believe me, old buddy," Monk looked at Charlie and winked, "from now on, it won't be so easy for them. In fact, Captain Peterson is going to make this district so hot for them they'll be afraid to show on any scene."

"You talk to Peterson already?"

"Naw, he's too high and mighty with his bullshit principals and morals. But I control his Black ass through Alderman Sanders." Monk tightened his Japanese robe, leaned back on his heels, and blew cigarette smoke toward the ceiling. He spoke again. "Yep, Big Jim keeps ole Peterson right in line!"

"Why don't we take care of those little punks and then we won't have to look over our shoulders?"

"Look, Charlie. We're supposed to play it smart. Why soil our hands when we can get someone else to do it?"

"Yeah . . . as usual, you're right."

"Just like before, Charlie. When they get it, we'll be miles away."

Jimmy, Charlie Dumont's kid brother, was walk-

THE BLACK CONNECTION

ing along 49th and Cottage Grove Avenue. He was accompanied by his little friend Sammy. The boys had just left school.

"What happened, man?" Jimmy asked.

"Aw, Mr. Shrock, the principal, had me down to his office. He wants me to bring a note explaining my absence, either that or bring my parents to school."

"Gee, I hope my teacher doesn't send me to the office. My brother Charlie would want to know why I've been absent."

"Come on, Jimmy. Let's go by Slappy's place. I sold two packs of smack during recess. I can pay Slappy what I owe him and still save a pack for you and me."

Traffic on Cottage Grove Avenue was indeed quite busy as the boys strolled along the sidewalk. At the corner of 47th Street, workers were laboriously constructing a project building; a frequent scene on Chicago's south side. Staccato sounds filled the air. Men on high scaffolds shook like jelly as automatic hammers connected a dream of steel. A mild September breeze blanketed the awesome city and the bright celestial globe slowly turned to the West.

"I thought," said Sammy, "that Mr. Shrock had heard about me selling stuff around the school."

"Boy, you really would have been in big

by Randolph Harris

trouble," Jimmy answered, loping along.

"But if I'm in school every day, I'll miss some of my customers around the pool hall," Sammy answered.

"Yeah, I guess you make more money around the pool hall than you do at school."

"You know I do, man."

"Let's hurry," Jimmy said. "I want to take a fix, then get on home."

The two teenage boys sauntered across 47th Street and darted into the mouth of the alley between Cottage Grove and Drexel Boulevard. About fifty feet up the alley, they quickly turned and entered a shabby yard in which patches of grass had sparsely grown. Leaving the yard, they hurriedly entered the mouth of the gangway, then stopped midway and knocked on a wooden door which had an iron gate with strong crisscrossed bars boldly stretched before it.

A slight and heavy voice answered, and then was heard a turning of locks. An Afro-head greeted Jimmy and Sammy. The man called Slappy let them in.

The ground level apartment loomed eerie with abstract paintings and lights of low multi-colored tones. Two shabby couches pushed together, back to back, divided the lightly furnished room. A small alcove led to three other cubicles and each

THE BLACK CONNECTION

held a bed.

This was one of Monk's shooting galleries. It was Charlie Dumont's job to make sure it maintained a constant supply of very diluted heroin. Slappy, in turn, would receive fifty percent of the proceeds for the disposing of it.

Slappy, bony-faced and exceedingly thin-bodied, handed Jimmy an old neck-tie. Jimmy Dumont, scrawnily built with diminutive brown eyes, placed one end of the neck-tie between his teeth and wrapped it tightly around his up-raised left arm. Slappy, quite helpfully, handed Jimmy a hypodermic needle. Jimmy Dumont aimed it at his arm.

chapter 7

AGENTS DANNY GRUFF and Sidney Miller were seated at a one way window in a serene, green and white house. It was located two entrances south and across the street from Oscar (Monk) Davis' new residence. The house which contained the agents displayed a "For Rent" sign on the front lawn.

A truck which bore a plumbing and electrical sign was parked in the driveway.

To be sure, the green house was not in the least conspicuous. The homes on each side of it also posted signs of vacancy on their front lawns; the result of fast-exiting whites.

Recently, the house had been acquired by the Federal Bureau of Narcotics for the immediate purpose of surveillance. A movie camera was meticulously angled at the window and Agent Miller vigilantly sat behind it; he was busily adjust-

THE BLACK CONNECTION

ing and peering through its high-powered zoom sight. Both seasoned agents wore brown, button-up overalls, on which was the title CORONET PLUMBING AND ELECTRICAL REPAIR.

Agents of the Bureau of Narcotics had had the Davis' home under clandestine observation from its second day of occupancy. Those agents included Ronald Monihan, who appeared to be a molded replica of Agent Danny Gruff. And there was Monihan's partner, Agent Jeffrey E. Boyd; he bore a striking resemblance to Agent Miller, who was of the other team.

It had been concluded and, in fact, declared by Chief Director Hines, that Monk's home should indeed have around-the-clock surveillance. The intricate strategy of the situation was to have at all times two of the four agents on twelve hour shifts. Arriving agents would drive a plain bureau car into the green and white garage, which was lodged in the rear—with their brown button-up overalls on, of course. Once relieved, the two housed agents would leave by the front door, enter the panel truck, and drive casually away; thus giving the appearance of completing an ordinary day's work, but actually leaving two agents in a supposedly empty house.

And of course, when the agents made their return in the panel truck, Agents Monihan and Boyd

by Randolph Harris

would go to the garage, retrieve their car, and leave from the rear.

Through the sight of the camouflaged movie camera, Agent Miller had an unobscured view of Monk's home: spacious green lawn, wide driveway, red brick structure trimmed in white stone; all of this zoomed within Miller's focus.

"When do you think he'll make his move?" Miller asked his partner, without moving his head.

"That's the fly in the buttermilk," Danny Gruff answered. "Noise has been shaking the town all week about the big shipment that's supposed to hit the city. The bastard's just gotta move!" Agent Gruff slammed the empty package to the floor, reached to his overall pocket and retrieved a fresh pack of cigarettes. He spoke again. "This shipment is too big. Monk's got to oversee it." Danny was pacing, and with a cigarette in hand, he was blowing a lot of smoke.

Miller silently continued his vigil.

Danny continued. "That fucking shipment left Haiti over a week ago. Those Interpol guys are very seldom wrong. We've just got to nail this guy." Danny appeared determined. "Sid, I know you can see it. Take that double murder down on 50th Street. Both bodies were bound and gagged—real execution style. Why after a while, the guy will think he's a Black Godfather; plus, there's definite indication of amalgamation with law enforcement. When people begin killing arbitrarily, the country's in a bad way, Sid."

"What about that Don's nephew, Bonito?" Miller asked, as he stepped away from the camera. "Do you think we'll get a chance to nail him?"

Agent Gruff replaced Miller behind the camera. "That's where we're gambling," Gruff answered. "The gamble is whether Don Serritelli will send his Capo, or send Bonito, his nephew. As you know, the Director indicated that all liaisons reported it real quiet out East."

"Humph," said Miller. "The quiet before the storm."

"Yeah," responded Gruff. "You're probably right. Everyone just waiting . . . including us!"

"And it's been an established fact," Miller said, "that the courier on that last pitch was Monk's wife. Right?"

"Right."

Miller walked around an oblong wooden table. A telephone decorated it. Two hand-sized walkie-talkies lay near the phone and two .38 magnum hand guns were also carefully placed. These items were presently the agents' working tools.

"Ah ha," Danny said, arching himself in the chair behind the camera. "I've got action."

"Is it Monk?" Miller stepped to the one way

by Randolph Harris

window.

"You struck out. It's a *she*," Danny replied.

"Who? . . . Sonya?"

"How many guesses do you want?" Agent Gruff was leaning forward. His head was glued to the camera sight. He raised his hand and quickly pressed a button on the side of the machine. A small red light glowed and there came a soft whirring sound.

"Looks as if the lady's been shopping," Danny said. "Boy, look at those boxes. She certainly knows how to spend Oscar's money."

Miller was gazing through the upper half of the window as Danny peered into the camera sight. "Monk must have been watching for her," Miller remarked.

"Yeah," said Danny. "I see he's opening the door." Agent Gruff reached the button and shut off the machine.

Miller lowered himself to his chair and Danny relaxed back in his, also.

"Oops! Here we go again." Danny's head went back into the sight. Miller was also on his feet.

"It's Monk," Gruff said. "He's leaving. Get on that talkie, Sid."

"Got'cha." Miller reached and began fingering the walkie-talkie button. "Calling field scooter! Calling field scooter, over."

THE BLACK CONNECTION

The call was answered by two field agents, Kenney and Myers, who were inconspicuously parked five blocks west on Stony Island Avenue.

Miller's voice was heard. "Target leaving house in black T-Bird; license plates R for Ruth, A for Arthur, Zero, One, Six, Five." Agent Miller leaned toward the window, peered, then spoke again. "Target's car heading north on Chandler." The field agents quickly confirmed the call, and both parties closed out.

Agent Gruff straightened. "Here, take over, Sid. I'm going to the john." Danny stretched his arms to the ceiling as he headed toward the small private enclosure.

Agents Kenney and Myers raced the Bureau car east on 95th Street. The black T-Bird was nowhere in sight. Agent Kenney was driving; he jerked the steering wheel left and both agents strained their vision as they passed slower cars.

Kenney, tall, white, and sharp featured, was very agile-minded. Myers, medium-height and square-faced, was number one in his karate class, and indeed quite rugged in tight clinches.

Myers rocked forward when Kenney abruptly slowed the Bureau car. Kenney had spotted a black car ahead. He steadied his car on the white line and focused on the plates ahead. RA 0165.

That was it. The license plate on the T-Bird

by Randolph Harris

ahead checked out.

Monk, in the black Bird, turned left at 79th Street. He took the angled South Chicago Avenue and headed west.

Agent Kenney and Myers, trailing at a reasonable distance, allowed the T-Bird a comfortable lead.

The black car was crossing Cottage Grove Avenue. It was passing the graveyard on 67th Street.

The two agents had been present at the last strategy grouping, and each recalled District Director Hine's attack speech. There had been superceding orders concerning the alarming of the top suspect: Monk.

A stop light had stilled the black T-Bird. A large diesel transport truck responded to straining gears and rumbled past; probably heading for the Calumet Expressway.

The light changed to green and the Bird was rolling again. It turned at Langley Avenue. The street displayed two and three story brick buildings, between which were stuck a few privately-owned frame houses. Monk braked the car in front of a brown frame house and shortly, he was ringing the door bell.

Agents Kenney and Myers had observed Monk's every move; they waited. Approximately three minutes had flown by when the door of the brown

THE BLACK CONNECTION

frame house opened again. Three persons, all Black, two males, and one young lady, stepped out onto the porch and then descended the wooden steps.

The agents became tense. Myers, seated on the passenger side, had an urge to slump. The experienced agents knew if they were spotted by any of the three, the occupants of the house would receive an urgent telephone call. Thus, Monk would instantly be alerted.

The September breeze was surprisingly brisk as the huddled trio ambled through the small yard. At the sidewalk they turned toward the agents. The two white agents sat motionless. Kenney stared; Myers mused. No agent cherished the thought of blowing the lid on a recon mission. It had become a proven fact that the unveiling of a tail could so drastically change prelaid strategy that its effects would be months in telling. This present dope case was too big to cause a foolish blow-up now.

The three persons were drawing closer. Myers, on the passenger side of the car, focused on dope-glazed eyes, sunken jaws, and that hard-to-forget dopefiend lope. That was it—a pad—possibly a shooting gallery. The three were within two cars of the parked narcotics agents'. They stopped at a blue sedan. All three entered and rode away.

Fifteen minutes had passed, according to Agent Kenney's watch. Two more people had entered the

by Randolph Harris

house and, as yet, Monk had not come out. It was indeed safe for the agents to assume that of the last two entries, both showed blatant signs of drugs.

Keeping in mind the Chief Agent's so recent get tough policy, Kenney and Myers would definitely recommend that the brown frame house on Langley Avenue be raided—Immediately!

Monk was leaving! Tall, and still swaggering, he entered the black T-Bird and steered away from the curb. Furtively, the agents trailed Monk and the T-Bird along Langley Avenue, through Washington Park, and then to a basement apartment on 52nd Street. The scenes of human traffic, to say the least, were quite similar. It was obviously another narcotics pad! Like the illicit one on Langley Avenue, the present establishment would be put into the agents' report for expedient siege.

Shortly, though longer than before, Monk returned. He drove through Washington and into Jackson Park and after cruising along Stony Island, he eventually arrived back home. Reaching Agents Gruff and Miller over their walkie-talkies, Agents Kenney and Myers closed out.

The next morning inside the green and white house, agents Monihan and Boyd had long since departed after working the night detail. Agent Miller was seated behind the movie camera. Agent Gruff, also seated, was talking. "According to

THE BLACK CONNECTION

Kenney and Myers' report, Monk never went near the tavern headquarters. Isn't it strange that he's staying so close to the house?"

"After getting a glimpse of Dolly, his little playmate, you're damn right it is." Miller twisted his head for a second, and then it was back to the camera.

"Could be he's waiting for a call," Gruff said. "An important one, if you know what I mean."

"Yeah, I'm with you."

"You know, Sid, it may also have to do with those shotgun killings a few nights ago. It's damn obvious that the killers were after Monk."

"Yeah, everyone knows that dark grey Olds. It's my bet it was those Black Angels. Hold it! . . . I've got action!" Miller pressed the camera button. The red indicator said ON. "Will you look at this?" Miller stated.

"What?" Gruff left his seat and stared through the one way window. "It's that Alderman guy, chauffeur and all. Damn it, I knew we'd regret not tapping that friggin' phone!"

"The Chief said that the Director in Washington was reluctant for some unknown reason. That's why we're on this 'Observe' detail," Miller said, as he watched Sonya come to the door and admit Big Jim Sanders.

"Bugged phones don't do much good with old

by Randolph Harris

pros like that ole geezer. They're so used to talking double, I'll bet he speaks Pig Latin in his sleep," Danny said.

Miller's eyes targeted on the shiny black sedan in which sat a Black chauffeur. The car was parked in the spacious driveway.

"How many coats of wax do you think that buggy has on it, Danny?"

"I don't know. But you can bet the taxpayers footed the bill. Damn, that didn't take long"

The plainly dressed chauffeur was holding the car door open for the cigar-puffing Alderman.

"He didn't bring anything and he didn't leave with anything. I agree with you, Danny Boy. The old guy doesn't trust telephones."

"I would like to be in on those raids tonight."

"You don't know. You may get your wish." Miller stretched his arms outward, leaned back and spoke again. "Come on, take over this neck-breaker."

Agent Gruff replaced Miller at the camera. "Well, the Chief put us all on *Alert*, so you know what that means." Danny didn't move his head from the camera. Miller was walking toward the john.

The two agents did not know, but at that very moment, narcotics agents armed with warrants had been dispatched from the Director's Office and had

THE BLACK CONNECTION

left the Fifth and Seventh District's Police Stations. There, the agents, as was customary, had asked for and received aid from the Chicago Police.

Captain Charles Sewicki, Commander of the Seventh District, had graciously supplied squads of men and two available paddy wagons.

Captain LaVerne Peterson, Commander of the Fifth District, had done likewise. The similarity, however, ended there. Captain Sewicki called his wife to explain that he would be late arriving home. Captain Peterson also made a call. Instead of calling his wife, Captain Peterson reached Alderman Big Jim Sanders at the Alderman's office and excitedly blurted out what was happening.

It would have surprised the agents had they known that Alderman Sanders had briefly considered using the telephone. But of course, it was imperative that Monk be immediately informed of the impending raids. Not one to hesitate when a bonus was promised him, Alderman Sanders rushed from his office and made a hurried trip to Davis' home. There, the seasoned politician hastily accepted his reward and departed.

Monk had let Big Jim out and closed the door. He then reclined on the luxurious sofa and picked up the phone. He dialed a number in New York City. Sonya was descending the stairs, and Monk, just finishing his conversation, hung up. "I just let

by Randolph Harris

Big Jim out," Monk said. "He told me that Peterson had wired him that some pads were about to be busted."

Sonya answered. "I saw his car backing out the driveway." Sonya's tall, lithe figure was outlined through her transparent negligee. She seated herself on the sofa beside her husband and crossed her legs, thigh over thigh. "Have you heard from Bonito yet?"

"Naw," Monk answered, "but I did make a call to New York. I need some help. Things are happening too damn fast. And concerning Bonito, I'm glad he hasn't called."

"Why?" Sonya asked twisting her head.

"Simply because I haven't got enough bread." Monk walked over to the expertly hung drapes. He pulled the cord and gazed out. The tranquil neighborhood lay dormant. Monk turned and faced his wife. "You know, I went out yesterday and collected from a few spots. Charlie had called earlier and told me about some pick-ups he'd made on the lower end."

"Oscar?" Sonya paused and looked down at her lap. She fingered a fringe on her negligee.

"Well, what is it?"

"Did you send for those two hit men?" Sonya lifted her gaze and stared at her husband.

The deep carpeting gave way as Monk pressed

THE BLACK CONNECTION

over the floor. He stopped a few feet in front of Sonya, then stared down at his wife. "You're damn right I did, and they'll be here tonight. Captain Peterson told Big Jim that there are Feds all over the south side. When these Agents start knocking over our galleries, eventually they'll find someone who's willing to talk. And you know, we can't afford that."

"Okay, okay," Sonya fluttered her hands and rose from the expensive sofa. Immediately, and without saying another word, she headed for the spiral stairs.

Monk returned to the large window and closed the drapes. Moments later Agents Gruff and Miller spotted a green dilapidated station wagon cruise slowly past the Davis' home. Agent Miller pressed the ON button and the movie camera purred.

Agents Kenney and Myers, being the instruments who had discovered the narcotics pads, were among the first agents chosen for the highly sensitive raids. They were accompanying a detail of agents to the brown house on Langley Avenue.

Inside the brown frame house, a telephone rang. Odell Jones, a light-complexioned Negro man, lifted the receiver. "Hello... Thanks, Oscar. Damn! They're already here!"

Odell, an ordinary-sized man, heard multiple footsteps on the wooden porch. The stash! He had

by Randolph Harris

to clean up! Instinctively he dashed to the pillow on the rumpled bed. Many times diluted for the strictly walk-in trade, two ounces of heroin were hastily removed. He also pocketed his snub-nose .38 pistol. Odell heard a commotion at the front door. He also heard his neighbor's dog barking in the rear. Engulfed with complexities, he had no time to rip the plastic coverings and flush the illicit drugs. Damn! He had only been home a year, and obviously couldn't afford another bust. The front door was caving in! That damn administration and its "No-knock" law!

The roof! Odell raced up the stairs to the upper bedroom. He would use the bedroom window and reach the roof! As if in unison, the front and back doors burst open.

Two uniformed policemen with drawn guns were the first to enter through the rear door. The splintered front door produced a mixture of uniformed and plainclothed custodians. Frantically, Odell raised the upstairs bedroom window.

A uniformed officer bounded the stairs with pistol poised. Odell could hear voices from downstairs. Once out the window, he scrambled to the roof and desperately eyed the roof of the apartment building beyond. Chancing a downward glance, the dope dealer saw the cars of officialdom parked on the street below. He crouched and ran

THE BLACK CONNECTION

forward. His stem-like legs took on muscular knots as he prepared to spring! The uniformed policeman had reached the window and shouted, "Stop! Police officer!" By that time Odell was in the air. Odell grasped the edge of the roof. He heard a shot! The pellet pounded the brick wall. He skinned himself atop the roof. Another shot! And then he bounded across and leaped onto the lower roof next door. Odell's tannish face was drenched with perspiration. He scrambled to the porch below. Confusion clouded the entire area. Shouts and commands were heard throughout the neighborhood.

Dogs barked frantically as Odell bounded down the stairs and across the back yard. He burst into the alley. A squad car was approaching. He ducked back, and desperately looked around. Odell bounded over the fence. There was a small flower bed. A large tree marred its horticultural outlay. Midget size hedges outlined the perimeter of the yard.

Odell lay flat. His head associated with the running roots of the tree. The smell of fresh earth overpowered the scent of sprouting buds. He heard the waxing tires of the squad car coming closer. He wondered if his pounding heart would divulge his hiding place.

The police car was now outside the yard, the car

by Randolph Harris

motor idling. Odell suddenly got an urge to jump up and run. He could feel the pressure of the gun in his pants pocket, but he dared not move. He cursed his body for wanting to breathe. The squad car finally moved on down the alley. Odell cautiously raised himself from the fertile soil. He was on his knees as he fingered into his pocket and grasped the snub-nose pistol. The butt of the gun felt cold and clammy.

Odell heard a noise behind him like the opening of a door. "What are you doing in my flower bed? Police! Help! Police!" A woman with rollers in her hair was screaming. She stood at the back door of the house. Odell panicked. He sprang from his knees and fired a shot in the direction of the screaming voice. Odell ran toward the gate that led into the yard and suddenly found himself in the alley. The police car—it was backing up! Odell dashed across the alley. One of the policemen had leaped from the squad car and his pistol was in his hand. Odell fired off two rapid shots in the direction of the blue uniform. He scrambled over the fence, but not before he saw the squad car stop and the policeman crumble to the ground.

Odell landed in a yard that had a small sand pile. A child's red tricycle lay on its side. A miniature wagon was in the dope peddler's path as he bounded toward the mouth of the gangway that

THE BLACK CONNECTION

was situated along the side of the apartment building.

Sirens were heard above voices of confusion. Dogs barked at intruders as the search was centered on the neighborhood back yards. Arriving at the opposite end of the gangway, Odell spied a laundry truck. He was in a crouch as he dashed between two cars. He paused. His entire body was drenched with sweat. His breath actually hurt his throat as his open mouth hurriedly pulled in air and immediately pushed it out again.

Rush hour traffic filtered through the streets, as the orange celestial globe sought a place to rest. Odell, bent low, crept to the laundry truck door and tried the handle. It was locked. A squad car was approaching. Odell plopped flat along the curb. Then he heard the deadliest of all sounds. The voice came out of the gangway from which he had just run.

The dogs, they were talking about those dreaded dogs! "Call that canine wagon and bring those dogs through here." A gold braided white policeman was speaking. The police lieutenant was holding a plastic packet. "He must have dropped this as he ran." Odell, lying flat and gripping the damp pistol, was tempted to pat his pocket, a gesture that could easily cause his discovery. But he did not stir.

The policeman re-entered the hollow of the

by Randolph Harris

gangway. Odell heard footsteps coming from behind. He raised himself to a half crouch. It was the laundry man. He almost dropped the bundle of clothes when Odell confronted him with the snubnose .38. It was quite simple for the frightened laundryman to enter the truck and drive away while Odell curled on the floor and aimed the pistol up at him.

Later that night news of the policeman who was shot in an alley had spread throughout the city. Monk was entertaining two out-of-town visitors. In fact, they were the same two men who had visited him only a few weeks before. And it can be said without any doubt that their homicidal assignment was the same. The clandestine conversation was interrupted by the ringing of the telephone. Monk answered it. Angrily his voice cracked.

"Damn it, man. What're you doing calling here? Every roller in town is looking for you. I thought you'd be long gone by now."

The two average-sized Black men who were visiting could not help noticing the anger on Monk's face, or how swiftly his voice changed. Suddenly it became tranquil and convincing. "I tell you what." Monk turned and looked at the two visitors. "Tell me where you are, and I'll send someone to help you right away. But look, Odell, after you get to

THE BLACK CONNECTION

the hideout, don't call me, just stay in touch with Charlie, okay? . . . Yeah, man, you know I'm going to send you some bread. Now, Odell, don't forget. Stay in touch, but do it through Charlie." Monk sighed and hung up the phone.

Monk looked at his two visitors and said, "Well, here's where you earn your first bread." He wrote an address on the reverse side of a small white card.

Monk gave the card to his two visitors.

chapter 8

THE WEATHER, for September, was exceedingly warm. For Jimmy Dumont, it was even hotter and more uncomfortable.

Jimmy Dumont had been suspended from school. Told twice by the teacher to bring his parents, he had not responded. Not to mention the previous days of absenteeisms, Jimmy had frequently been caught asleep in his classes.

Jimmy mused quite a bit about his present critical situation. The unbearable pains were, in fact, tying his stomach into knots. This thing of misery and humiliation, to say the least, had imprisoned his entire mental and physical structure. To begin, it all had appeared as mere folly.

THE BLACK CONNECTION

Casually missing a day at the gym had really created no self concern, and those days that were spent at the pool hall could readily be cast off as just a waste of time. But wait! ... The pool hall! Yes, it was the pool hall where he had received his first invitation to this now lecherous addiction. Jimmy focused quite vividly on the incident.

Sammy—no, it was Alonzo, a former classmate—had invited Jimmy to accompany them in this newly found sensation. More through curiosity than anything else, Jimmy had joined Sammy and Alonzo on the journey to the old condemned apartment building. It was located a half block from the pool hall.

Jimmy recalled how reluctant he had become when at first they entered the half-demolished abode. Sammy had given out with laughter while Alonzo gave forth an utterance of "Chicken." Clearly, Jimmy could have stated that both boys' expressions were wrong. It was ostensibly the condition and eeriness of the dilapidated structure that had brought Jimmy's hesitancy.

Jimmy recalled the dust-laden planks that were once referred to as floors; steps were missing from stairs, doors were missing from portals, windows showed jagged panes, and some showed no panes at all. Digested waste that scurrying rats had obviously avoided was something to be watched for.

by Randolph Harris

Had Jimmy Dumont chosen to utter excuses, indeed he could have readily done so. He, however, followed with docility, and assured himself that he was too strong for any mishaps.

It was in the filth-crowded enclosure which once was a bedroom that Jimmy Dumont, quite unknowingly, signed a death pact with heroin.

Now Jimmy was crossing 47th at Cottage Grove Avenue. He had to make it to Slappy's pad. It seemed as though every muscle of his body ached excruciatingly. At last he reached the yard, entered the mouth of the gangway, stuck his scrawny arm through the iron bars and, very weakly, he knocked on the door.

Slappy peered out, then busily began to unlock his shooting gallery. Jimmy, perspiring quite freely, entered.

At the perimeter of the city limits, in an old deserted warehouse on South Chicago Avenue near Chicago's last liquor store, Odell paced the concrete floor. Had the mixture been yielding, he could have easily worn a path.

Odell stood at a window on the second floor in the old warehouse. In the past, he had frequented the place quite often. But of course, that was in its more lucrative days. The help, consisting mostly of drivers, would consistently have weekend crap

THE BLACK CONNECTION

games, which repeatedly proved vastly profitable for Odell. Indeed, it was to his sadness that Odell learned of the warehouse's demise.

Odell turned from the cracked dirty window and retraced his steps. Looking over the place, Odell saw dressers with three legs and some with two. Beds with headposts and nothing else, chairs with backs and no seats, mirrors on the floor instead of the wall. The majority of these furnishings were shattered.

Puffs of dust appeared as smoke from the perpetual tread of Odell's feet. There also were two movable platforms, each about two feet high. Both were constructed on rollers. Probably forgotten in despondent haste. Lights from the Calumet Expressway cast an unremitting glow by which the warehouse became briefly illuminated during the passing of each car.

Odell was back at the window. After looking once, he turned, then turned back again. A car was coming down the ramp of the busy Expressway. The frightened dope peddler leaned very close to the wall as he watched through the cracked window. He saw two neatly dressed Black men alight from the car. Years of ghetto awareness came to Odell's aid; they were not homeguards! They were not police! Their dress, their walk, their complete style. They were hit men!

by Randolph Harris

Computerized thoughts laced through Odell's cranium, and only one answer came forth loud and clear! He had been crossed. So cleverly crossed by a dirty motherfucker called Monk.

Odell felt to his belted .38 snub-nose pistol. He checked it. His life depended on just three bullets. He heard the seldom-used door downstairs squeak and whine as it was forced to break its pattern. Odell dashed behind a dormant dresser, then he crouched. Gritty dust coverings on the concrete stairs told of stealthy footsteps.

Passing headlights from the expressway cars flashed through the warehouse blackness. The footsteps were very near the top of the stairs. The lights—the passing headlights! When the headlights passed, they illuminated the immediate side of the warehouse. Odell darted to an old dismantled couch. Twisted wire and cotton protruded from it. He had to reach the opposite side of the room. It was imperative that he gain the advantage.

Two men—probably pros. Three bullets. There could be no miss. Odell spied an old ice box and started his dash. The two assassins had reached the top of the steps. They saw him!

Odell dived back behind the seedy couch. He heard two zipping sounds and witnessed the jagged impact upon the couch. Silencers! They were pros, all right!

THE BLACK CONNECTION

Odell saw one of the movable platforms at the opposite end of the old couch. He knew the killers' eyes were not yet accustomed to the warehouse blackness. Where in the hell are those passing cars? Odell needed those headlights badly. A car was coming; he could see the expressway through the cracked window pane. The glow was becoming larger, larger! Lying on his back, the desperate dope peddler gave the platform a tremendous push with both feet.

Iron wheels on which the platform was mounted made loud sounds as it thundered over the cemented floor. The killers were in confusion. Headlights from the passing cars instantly illuminated two well-dressed Black men who were engulfed by the complexities of noise and light. An ominous gun showed in each one's hand. Odell raised and fired twice! A human cry of anguish was in unison with falling furniture. The headlights vanished, and again there was blackness.

Only one bullet left, but Odell was sure that he now had only one adversary. The impasse was broken by two zipping sounds immediately followed by two gashing thuds into the shabby couch.

Yes, one of the would-be assassins was very much alive. Odell thought frantically. If only he could ice this last dude, things would be quite beautiful for number one. He could perhaps lay

by Randolph Harris

odds and win that the car driven to the warehouse had recently been stolen. It would, however, provide an excellent means of escape.

Odell's eyes became equated to a cat's in this almost tar-like darkness. But of course it was a must. Didn't his precious life depend upon it?

Odell's vision settled upon the old icebox, and there the other rolling platform was innocently resting.

No, the would-be killer, by his ever present silence, had proved himself a pro; and pros don't go for the same trick twice. But wait! Odell thought as he hugged the filthy floor. His nostrils became polluted with stale and grimy odors. Maybe he could use the same trick, but this time only as a diversionary tactic. The passing headlights were only illuminating the opposite side of the warehouse, and after witnessing his companion's fatal mistake, the crafty killer would definitely not reveal himself. Especially not during the passing of cars.

Odell, desperate, scared, and grimy with dirt from a flower bed, prepared to make his move. Cars were coming. Odell saw the glow on the windows grow larger. He tensed himself. The rays of the headlights hit the far corner of the warehouse. Odell was ready. He quickly dove behind the ice box and glued his body to the floor.

THE BLACK CONNECTION

There was still no sound or movement from the other side. Odell was now on the same side of the room, only the icebox concealed him. And so, left with only one bullet, he had to get close and make damn sure of his target.

Odell shoved the platform with all his might and moved at the same time. There was a climactic crash as the rolling platform came to an abrupt halt. Odell heard no other sound or movement. He was dealing with a fox. He also knew that he was now within a few feet of his deadly foe, but he needed those passing lights just one more time.

This was it: do or die. The next car that passed would briefly illuminate both men. Therefore he, Odell, must use the element of surprise and shoot first. Hardly had the thought fled his brain, when reflecting light invaded the room. Odell was lying flat with his pistol poised.

Piercing light knifed through the blackness and there, not six feet in front of Odell, was a crouched Black man. The man was actually facing him when Odell squeezed off his one and only shot. He saw a crimson hole appear in the man's forehead, but it was simultaneous with two zipping sounds that came from the ominous weapon that was held by the dying man. Odell immediately felt the impact. It raised him from the dirty floor. He desperately tried to open his eyes, but his eyelids simply

by Randolph Harris

could not enlist the strength. He stubbornly rolled over and died.

Headlights from the passing cars continued by, unknowingly instrumental in the deaths of three men.

At 51st Street, Charlie Dumont and his mother proceeded from the entrance of the Provident Hospital. Charlie had his arm around the weeping woman. Little Jimmy Dumont was dead. The cause of death was due to an overdose.

It had started raining and the drive to the Dumont's apartment was woefully sad as Charlie guided the car. He was still in a state of profound shock.

They were in the apartment when Mrs. Dumont gave vent to her feelings and shook with a convulsion of tears. Sitting on the side of the bed, she squinted up at her only remaining son. "Charlie, tell me. Tell me how a thing like this could happen to my baby?"

"I don't know, Mama. The doctor told me that someone had brought Jimmy to the emergency waiting room and left him there."

"But..." Mrs. Dumont tried to restrain her tears. "But how could dope kill my son? He didn't use dope, did he, Charlie? Did he?"

"Aw, Ma," Charlie turned his back to his

THE BLACK CONNECTION

mother. He couldn't force back the tears. "I'll find out." Charlie's voice rang with a terrifying finality.

Mrs. Dumont sat up straight on the edge of the bed. Her face was like wet cement, though the flow of tears had stopped. Through clenched teeth, she spoke. "Yeah, you find out, and when you do, kill him, Charlie. Kill him, kill him, like he killed my Jimmy. Pump that poison into his arm. Pump it, pump it, pump it till he's dead like Jimmy!"

The grey-haired woman leaned to the bed and her tears overflowed like a dam. Her repeated convulsions caused the bed to shake.

"Aw, Ma." Charlie, with dampened eyes, walked over to the bed, and with a hand on his mother's trembling shoulder, he tried to console her.

"Charlie." The old lady's wet face looked of smooth leather immediately after a tanner's finish. "Who would give Jimmy dope? I hear people always talking about the white folks killing Black people one way or another. But Charlie, the only white folks Jimmy knew were those at his school."

"I know, Ma." Charlie looked at the ceiling and gritted his teeth. The tears did not come.

"No, you don't know, Charlie." Mrs. Dumont straightened. She was gripping the sleeves of Charlie's sport jacket with both hands. "You don't know who these people are. If you did, you and other Black people would get them from around

by Randolph Harris

us. You see, son, I know that Black people killed my boy. Didn't no white folks do it."

The factuality of her statement immediately dawned on Dumont. Apparently the sudden trauma of his brother's death had blocked a horrible realization. It probably was the outfit's dope! Dumont mused, then loudly exclaimed, "Oh, my God!"

Charlie Dumont instantly released himself from his mother's grasp, then fled to the bathroom and closed the door.

Proving that mothers are talented in the art of extending an abundance of love, Mrs. Dumont's heart went out to her overwrought son. A few moments passed and Dumont stepped from the private enclosure. His mother pitifully confronted him. "Charlie, do you think that those numbers people you work for might help us find the person who gave Jimmy the dope?"

"Mama, stop it! Stop it!"

"But can't you see, son? We've got to find out who these people are. People who go around and give kids dope are less than human. Why, they need to be ... I just can't think of anything that's bad enough for them."

Charlie Dumont looked down at his mother's tear-drenched face, then turned and entered his room. His mother surmised that he was filled with

THE BLACK CONNECTION

grief, and rightly so.

Once inside the room, Dumont recalled the narcotic charge that had eventually sent him to prison. He had sworn to his mother at that time that the charge was clearly a frame. It now was a blatant fact that the drugs from which his brother had died were undoubtedly distributed by he, himself, Charlie Dumont.

Where else could Jimmy have possibly come by dope? Every ounce of drugs sold in and around the immediate district was distributed by the Black outfit.

chapter 9

THE SCENE WAS MILES AWAY on an estate in New York's Staten Island. It was the well protected home of Don Santino Serritelli. The entrance was an electric gate which divided a long iron and concrete fence. Two massive Dobermans roamed the spacious greens at will. A hundred feet from the gate, a sentry house sat atop a small knoll. The dogs and gate were controlled by a guard from this point.

The spiraling driveway led to a rather expensive circular red brick mansion which was rumored to boast ten bedrooms. Though the grounds surrounding it bore well-manicured hedges, none of this foliage was rooted near the house. A half moon porch attempted to encircle the structure. Inside the house itself, things appeared conservatively

THE BLACK CONNECTION

chosen. High backed chairs placed atop Oriental rugs, and a bust of Napoleon decorated the wheel-shaped hall. From the alcove's particularly high ceiling hung a handcut glass chandelier and, of course, it reeked of Italian design.

Don Serritelli, looking rather sagacious, sat behind a large glass-topped desk in his study. A man of average height with dark grey-streaked hair which was obviously coal black at one time, Serritelli's hand was on his chin as he rested his square-shaped face. He was toying with a small curved scar; a reminder of earlier days on the historical waterfront.

His Consigliori, Mario Fanazi, sat facing him. Rather paunchy with an amiable round face which was topped by a shock of mixed grey wavy hair, he listened to the Don quite attentively.

"You may be correct, my Consigliori, but to send Capo Masoni on the trip would deprive my nephew Bonito of the much needed experience. Besides, with this Gano affair, you need Masoni here."

"This Black man Monk, you trust?" Fanazi asked.

"I know what you are saying. It is true they are rumored to be a weak people. Surely not of the blood of the Sicilians. But this man Monk came to me with the high recommendation of my old Capo

by Randolph Harris

friend, Guido Spilini, and from that time, he has proven himself an honorable man."

Seeing that his Don had already made the decision in question, Fanazi tempered his voice in making his final pitch. "Has the Don not heard that this man is having trouble with his own kind? And that he spoke falsely concerning money that Bonito paid two assassins for him?"

Don Serritelli spun in his swivel chair and gazed through the study window. "Again it is true what you say, but to me it was the sign of a man who is proud. He doesn't want us to think that he is incapable of controlling his own. Does my Consigliori fail to recall the earlier battles we had with the Gillianos, the DeStafanis, and not to mention the worrisome Ganos. Yes, my old friend, I am aware of these things. That is why I trust this Black man."

There was a knock on the study door. Bonito Serritelli was given permission to enter. After giving respect to his uncle, Bonito stepped in front of Fanazi and extended both hands downward. Fanazi extended his upward; the hands clasped.

"Fanazi, ole friend," Bonito uttered.

"You look good," Fanazi returned.

"I am returning from long business trip," Bonito said.

"Yes, I know," Fanazi answered. "And it was

THE BLACK CONNECTION

pleasant and profitable, I hope?"

"The business, it go fine," Bonito pointed out. "The profits will come later."

Don Serritelli said, "We were discussing that shipment to those Blacks in Chicago. Since you have been chosen to oversee it, what do you think? It is a very large order for them, you know."

Hunching his shoulders and flicking his hands, Bonito answered, "It okay wit me. You make plan, I follow instructions. Everything go fine."

Consigliori Fanazi looked at Don Serritelli and instantly knew it was not the answer the Don was expecting. He also realized that if Don Serritelli, who was childless, was wishing someday for Bonito to become a Don, the hope was rather dismal.

"Who do you plan to send with Bonito?" Fanazi asked, realizing that the assignment was usually given to a Capo regime who in turn was always accompanied by two soldiers.

Don Serritelli crossed his legs, knee over knee, and looked to the ceiling. "I had thought of Grassi and Tony. How do the names ring to you, Bonito?"

Fanazi sensed that the Don was bestowing on Bonito his rightful responsibility, for it was on the two soldiers that Bonito's life and freedom could very well depend.

"Oh, they suit me fine. Both of them I like,"

by Randolph Harris

Bonito answered, expressing with his hands.

Again Bonito had blundered with his answers and Don Serritelli could not let this one pass. "In this business it is not who you like, my nephew, but who is most fitted for the assignment. What say you about my choice, Fanazi?"

"They are both stalwart and dependable men," Fanazi answered. "The choices couldn't be better."

"Then it is settled," Don Serritelli pointed to Bonito. "You will call Oscar Davis and invite him to the racetrack to watch two horses that I own. They should be running at Windsor Racetrack two nights from now."

It was the next day in Chicago, at the home of Oscar (Monk) Davis. Monk was sitting in the breakfast nook; the maid had just placed his coffee. "Tell Mrs. Davis to come downstairs and join me, Mabel."

"Yes, Mr. Davis." The maid left immediately, heading for the stairs.

Shortly, dressed in a pink negligee, Sonya joined her husband, and the two sat and conversed.

"Do you think," Sonya asked, "that they'll connect you with the death of Odell and those other guys?"

"No chance," answered Monk. "That's a dead issue. You know Bonito finally called?"

THE BLACK CONNECTION

"It's about time. It's been over two weeks now," Sonya responded.

"Yeah, but you know how those things can happen."

"The funeral for little Jimmy was very sad, wasn't it?"

"Yes, it was," Monk answered. "I think it will be quite some time before Charlie gets over it."

Sonya, looking exceptionally sexy with her bulging breasts bursting from her low cut negligee, seemed to be pondering. "Oscar, did you ever get those books back from Charlie?"

"No, I didn't. I've been keeping records in some new books. Why?"

"Oh, I was just thinking."

"Well, you don't have to think too much about Charlie. But if you figure it best, I'll have him bring them over. In fact, I'll call him now."

Monk reached for the phone and dialed. Sonya busied herself pouring a fresh cup of coffee while her husband talked. She waited as Monk recradled the receiver.

"Like I said, you don't have to worry about Charlie. He'll bring the books later this evening."

"At least I'll feel better. When are you leaving for Detroit?"

"I will leave tomorrow morning, and you will leave tomorrow evening. We'll have to be extra

by Randolph Harris

careful carrying such a large amount of bread."

"How do you plan on doing it?."

"Aw, it won't be any problem. I'll take half with me and you can bring the other half."

"Gee, a half million dollars! Have you got it all together?"

"Almost. We're only short about fifty thousand. Charlie and I are making some pick-ups tonight."

While Sonya and her husband were conversing inside the house, a dark green station wagon drove by the outside of the house for the second time.

The two agents in the green and white house across the street pressed a button and filmed it all.

Later that night, lights in Chief Agent Ralph E. Hines' assembly room were still bright. They were having a grouping. As to be expected, Chief Hines was at the head of the long table. Ten proficient agents, equally divided, sat obediently and listened to him.

"Gentlemen, I am glad to say we have had some success in the Black Connection case. Interpol has informed us that they have located the landing field and jumping off point of the narcotics smugglers, and they have also assured the Department that the perpetrators would surely be apprehended. However, since it is now an established fact that Don Santino Serritelli masterminded the operation,

THE BLACK CONNECTION

Interpol has promised to delay their seige until we all can coordinate, thus avoiding a tipoff to individuals here in the States."

A rather clean cut redhead agent got the Chief Agent's attention. "What is it, McCall?" Chief Hines asked.

"If we apprehend the suspects in Canada, as your prelaid plans suggest," the redheaded agent asked, "in what territory will the suspects be tried?"

"The United States and Canada," Hines indicated, "have always cooperated with each other in these territorial matters. The suspects will be tried in the territories where the crime or crimes have been committed. And I'm sure we shall be able to prove that these narcotics, though hopefully confiscated in Canada, also have been distributed in the United States. Plus, we expect to have the cooperation of agents from the International Police when we apprehend the suspects."

Chief Hines walked over to the blackboard and began to draw a diagram. "If the suspects follow their previous pattern," Hines continued, "we will react as follows."

The group session lasted another hour before the agents were dismissed.

Charlie Dumont was seated in Monk's large

by Randolph Harris

living room when he spoke. "But, Monk, I tell you it has to be the same station wagon, man. Why, even last night when I was picking up this bread, I noticed it on two occasions." Dumont had pointed to an ordinary attache case.

Monk strolled across the lavishly furnished room and gazed through the curtained window. He turned and faced Dumont. "If it was the same station wagon that these witnesses have said they've seen leaving the scenes of the murders, how did they find out where I lived so fast?"

"Well, Monk, just like we have our ways of finding out certain things, I guess they also have theirs."

"I guess you're right, Charlie, but those fuckers can create quite a problem right now. You know we're supposed to leave sometime today."

"No, I didn't know."

"I didn't tell you last night because I didn't have things completed at the time. But Bonito will be in Detroit tonight at Windsor Raceway."

"So we leave today, huh?" Dumont didn't portray the elation that Monk had expected.

"What's wrong, man? I thought the news should give you a boost. On second thought, I'm sorry, ole buddy. It's still Jimmy, isn't it?"

"Aw, I don't know, Oscar. Maybe it is and maybe not. I just can't get myself together. I did

THE BLACK CONNECTION

have a lot of plans for that little guy."

Monk sat on the sofa beside Dumont. He reached out and patted Charlie on the knee. "I know how you feel, partner. It'll take time; just a little time." Monk's expression changed; he displayed a smile. "But in the meantime, we've got to make some bread, ole buddy." He slapped Charlie on the back. "Now come on, man, and help me outwit these punks. I can have them straightened out when we get back. But right now, our problem is to get out of the city with all this bread."

Charlie Dumont appeared to come out of his stupor; at least momentarily. "That's what I've been trying to tell you, Oscar. Those young dudes are hawking us like crazy, man!"

Monk got up and walked back to the window. He obviously was more concerned than he displayed. He poked a finger in the crack of the curtains and cautiously stared out. He turned back and faced Dumont. "I think I have a plan that will confuse them. That is, if they are stashed someplace watching."

Monk looked at his watch, and then he looked back at Dumont. "Tell you what. It's about three hours before our plane leaves. Suppose we leave the house carrying no bags and take a cab to the airport. We'll be back tomorrow morning anyway. They won't hardly make their move while we're in

by Randolph Harris

the cab. We can go directly to the airport. The move would take them by surprise.

Monk waited for Charlie's answer.

"Yeah," Dumont answered. "But what about the bread? How'll we get the bread?"

"Well," Monk was fingering his chin. "I was going to have Sonya bring half of it, but now I'll just have her bring another bag and carry all the bread. It's you and me the punks are after, not her."

"Sounds okay." Charlie was slightly phlegmatic.

Not too much later, Agents Gruff and Miller were still not alone. In fact, the relief agents, Monihan and Boyd, as yet had not left.

Gruff spoke. "The chief said that we should follow them whenever and wherever, even if it's to China."

Agent Ronald Monihan walked out of the toilet in time to ask, "Are Kenney and Myers still holding?"

"They should be," Miller said. "I'll check." Agent Miller was standing closest to the table. He picked up one of the pocket-sized walkie-talkies. "Calling Field Scooter, calling Field Scooter."

Miller released the talkie button and immediately received an answer. "Field Scooter, Myers."

"Miller here—just checking for location."

THE BLACK CONNECTION

"Hi, Sid, we're on 91st at Stony Island Avenue. Are we scheduled for action?"

"Your guess is as good as ours," Miller told him through the talkie. "Oh yeah," Miller continued, "what about that green wagon? Did you guys spot it when it rolled by last night?"

A second of static, then a clear channel.

"Yeah," Myers indicated, "it parked on 90th Street for forty-five minutes or so and then left. Don't worry, we've got the area covered."

"Okay, boy, over and out." Miller replaced the talkie. "Well, we're all on ice, but something tells me it won't be long."

Agent Boyd turned toward the one way window and stared out over Agent Gruff's shoulders. "I know the Chief is seldom wrong," he said, "but these double shifts can become real boring."

"It doesn't give you much time to investigate the fairer sex, huh, Jeff?"

Ronald Monihan looked at his partner and smiled.

"I didn't know you liked girls, Jeffy Boy." Miller, in shirt sleeves, hesitated lighting his cigarette to throw the crack at Agent Jeffrey Boyd.

"All right, can it, you guys, we've got action."

Gruff's head was pressing the camera sight. Miller and Boyd rushed to the window and the two peered through the upper half while leaning over

by Randolph Harris

Agent Gruff's shoulders. Agent Danny Gruff pressed the ON button and straightened. "Come on, Boyd, you and Monihan take over. Sid and I are taking your car."

"Here's the keys. It's parked in the garage out back," Boyd answered as he bent and slid behind the purring instrument.

"That's Monk and Dumont. They're getting into a cab," remarked Miller.

"Come on, Sid, unglue it and let's move!" Gruff prompted Miller as he headed for the rear door and the garage. He turned, holding the door knob. "Say, Moni, get Kenney and Myers on the talkie, tell them to keep that house pegged, and to look out for that green wagon. Something tells me it's up to no good."

"Gotcha, Danny." Monihan was reaching for the walkie-talkie.

"Come on, Sid," Agent Gruff repeated, "I think this is it."

"I hope so," Miller remarked as he donned his coat and followed his partner. The agents' black car, bearing Colorado license plates, proceeded from the alley on 89th Street, and they spied the yellow cab a half block away heading north on Jeffrey Boulevard.

"Well, what do you think, Danny?" Miller looked at his partner and then back to the car

THE BLACK CONNECTION

ahead.

"I don't know, Sid, but the Chief said we could expect the big move at any moment. This may be it."

"But, Dan, those guys are definitely up to some shit. And if this is the big pitch to meet Bonito, where is their luggage?" Miller appeared perturbed.

"We'll see, Sid, we'll see."

The yellow cab continued along Jeffrey Boulevard and spilled into Lake Shore Drive. Along with other cars, the agents' black car passed Jackson Park Beach and then the 50th On The Lake Motel. It was nearing the fabulous McCormick Place when it followed the yellow cab up the ramp and curved onto the Adlai Stevenson Expressway. Very shortly it trailed the cab into the very active Dan Ryan. It now was passing historic Maxwell Street, which was justifiably called Jew Town: street of the many wagons and twice as many bargains.

"Damn it, they're heading for the airport! This is it! Sid, this is it!"

Extraordinary jubilance showed on Agent Gruff's face. "I'll get the Chief on the phone; he'll get us two seat priority on the same plane. Shit, I'd ride up front with the pilots if need be!"

"We'll nail 'em, Dan, don't worry." Miller seemed slightly aroused by his partner's enthusiasm.

by Randolph Harris

The yellow cab was heading north when it moved from the center lanes and joined the airport traffic to the right. Agent Gruff was smiling when he replaced the dashboard telephone. Unlike before when they were forced to call ahead and have the dope dealers tailed; this time Agent Gruff was glad that he and his partner would have the final pleasure.

Lights from beyond gave evidence of the airport's presence. Drones from planes above was proof that it was rightly called the world's busiest: O'Hare Airport. The cabbie let the two dope dealers out.

The agents, unable to find a parking place, abandoned the black car, leaving it quite vulnerably situated. Then they rushed off.

"Hold it, Dan; we don't want to tip our mitts, do we?" Miller restrained his partner, who was really his superior, but at present was displaying an overly developed amount of zeal.

Becoming aware of his own persistence, Gruff said, "Thanks, Sid. It's just that we've put in so much time trying to tag these birds, I must have lost myself for a minute."

People were ambulating throughout the terminal. Stewardesses with fashion-model bodies and movie star profiles could easily be distinguished. Some people of importance were mixed with those

THE BLACK CONNECTION

of minor station.

Oscar (Monk) Davis and Charlie Dumont halted at the reservations counter. A rather clean-cut, youthful lad waited upon them. As the two Black men left the counter, Agent Gruff approached the young reservations clerk and furtively presented his folder. The young man calmly reached for a nearby phone, and momentarily he wrote out two slips of paper and handed them to Agent Gruff.

"We haven't got a sham bag this time, Dan." Miller was speaking in retrospect about the last time he and Gruff had tailed these same two Black men to this same airport.

"To hell with a sham bag," Gruff remarked, his eyes never straying far from his moving targets.

The plane was aloft. Agent Sidney Miller was sitting midway in the plane beside an elderly lady who, from her conversation, was going to Detroit, Michigan to visit her daughter. Agent Danny Gruff was sitting farther back next to an advertising executive who owned branches in Chicago and Detroit. Though the paunchy man's conversation to Gruff was exceedingly boring, the agent maintained an assumed interest.

Monk and Dumont were sitting together near the front of the plane.

After slicing through clouds that often took on images, the plane lowered its nose at Detroit's

by Randolph Harris

Metropolitan Airport. It was then late evening.

In the cab Monk was talking. "If any of those Black Angels dug us leaving the house, they would never figure on us leaving the city. I left word for Mickey to drive Sonya to the airport."

"Naw, I don't reckon they would," Dumont responded casually.

The apathy in Dumont's voice, of course, did not go unnoticed by Oscar Davis. That is to say, the real Oscar Davis; the man who, in only a few turbulent years, had built a Black organization which had been widely heard of and often feared, and less often whispered about and discreetly shunned.

Monk's astute brain took on objectionable thoughts toward his lifetime companion. But, no. It couldn't be as his ominous visions had materialized them to be. Hadn't Charlie brought back the books? It would be quite unforgettable if the situation were to bring about Dumont's sudden elimination.

The cab stopped at the Book Hilton Cadillac Hotel, and, like before, a fabulous suite was awaiting the two dope dealers.

Mickey, with a head of freshly processed hair, parked his car in front of Monk's fabulous home. He did not block the driveway because he was driving Sonya to the airport in Monk's new T-Bird; and it was parked there. Mickey, short and black, rang the doorbell.

"Hi, Mick." Sonya, looking immensely jazzy in a blue trimmed in white slack suit, opened the door and admitted him. "Come on in, I'll be ready in a second." She was busying herself with last-minute packing.

"We've got an hour before your plane leaves," Mickey replied, "so don't rush yourself."

"But the airport is quite a distance and I can't afford to be late."

Mickey, musing to himself, wondered if that was the case. Why wasn't she ready? The thought, however, was not expressed.

"Here, you take this bag and that one; I'll carry this other one on the plane with me." Sonya had pointed to the man's set of matching red leather bags. The one she carried was of alligator and a feminine design.

"Damn! Excuse me, Sonya, but I had no idea they were so heavy." Mickey grasped the bags, one in each hand, and followed Sonya to the side door which led to the driveway and the T-Bird. Sonya held the door open as Mickey wobbled through. She handed him the car keys, went back, secured the house door and then returned to the car.

Mickey twisted the ignition key and the T-Bird

by Randolph Harris

responded. He drove out along the driveway and was heading for the street. Sonya, sitting beside Mickey with an inward readiness for the unexpected, saw it first.

A dark green station wagon screeched to a halt and blocked the driveway. It appeared quite suddenly, as though out of nowhere. A side door of the station wagon flew open! A bushy-haired youth balanced a double-barreled shotgun. He was on one knee.

Even though she was amazed that anyone was aware of the money, Sonya assumed that it was a heist. Monk had instructed her to give the .45 automatic to Mickey, but only after she was safely to the airport. She moved just in time. A loud, fiery explosion flew from the mouth of the shotgun. Sonya, however, had opened the car door and rolled onto the driveway. The windshield of the T-Bird instantly disappeared, as did Mickey's entire head. Another bushy-haired youth leaped from the front of the station wagon and threw a Molotov cocktail. It traveled through the jagged hole where the windshield had once been. The T-Bird was immediately engulfed in flames.

Sonya was stretched prone along the edge of the driveway. She had retrieved the .45 automatic pistol from the pocket of her slack suit.

The youth standing in the driveway was handed

another Molotov by the third lad who was behind the steering wheel.

The money! The money! Sonya could not allow them to take the money. It represented all that she had ever planned for, schemed for, and quite frequently gone along with murder for. Because of this feeling what followed was a most incredible sight. The woman stood quite straight as she ran toward her attackers. Her automatic weapon belched forth death with every pull of her finger. She was balancing the gun with both hands when one of the bullets found its target in the head of the Molotov thrower. Another target and this time it was the driver.

There came two loud explosions, one from the muzzle of the double-barreled shotgun, and unfortunately Sonya was its target. The other explosion was what usually happens when the intense heat from flames contacts gasoline. The once new T-Bird was now merely a twisted, smoldering frame. Force from the T-Bird's explosion knocked the shotgun carrier back into the station wagon and sparks from the demolished car landed among a few Molotovs that had been thoroughly prepared, but until then unlit. The sparks lighted them.

It was the third and last explosion. A few persons had gathered and among the horrified spectators were Agents Kenney and Myers. And in the

by Randolph Harris

green and white house across the street, Agents Monihan and Boyd had filmed it all. It all happened so spontaneously there was nothing anyone could do.

Then another puzzlement crept into the immediate holocaust. An undetermined amount of burnt currency was scattered about the driveway and spacious lawn. Agents Kenney and Myers promptly received aid from Agent Boyd and the three agents guarded the area until the I.R.S. agents arrived.

chapter 10

THE BEIGE SHAG CARPET began to show paths as Oscar (Monk) Davis paced back and forth. He had called back and received the traumatic news. It was almost unbelievable, and yet it was quite true. Dumont stared at him as Monk's footsteps formed an oblong necklace in the floor.

"What are you going to tell Bonito?" Dumont's question sounded like a mountain of boulders at the beginning of a great rock slide.

Monk stopped pacing. He appeared to be looking at Charlie, or was he? It was really hard to say, due to the alien focus that Monk's eyes had presently taken.

"What will I do? What will I do? Tell me, Charlie, what will I do?" Monk's voice was barely above a whisper; his broad shoulders had seemingly become rounded and slumped.

Charlie Dumont watched this transfiguration

THE BLACK CONNECTION

with little concern. "I don't rightly know, Oscar. You've always told me, remember?"

"Maybe he'll give me the stuff on consignment. You think so, Charlie?"

"A half million dollars, Oscar?"

The telephone rang. It rang again and Charlie looked at Monk who was staring at the phone as though it was something mystical. "Aren't you going to answer it, man?" Charlie asked his friend.

Monk made zombie-like steps as he crept toward the vibrating instrument. After a couple of futile gestures, he lifted the receiver. "Hello, huh, yeah, yeah, yeah, Bonito, come on up." Monk fumbled with the receiver.

Charlie was trying to grasp the factuality of his friend's woe. Which was it that forlorned Monk more, the loss of the money, the loss of his wife, Sonya, or the confrontation with Bonito Serritelli? It could have been Dumont's excessive imagination, but to him it appeared that Monk was mindless of Sonya's untimely demise.

The doorbell rang and Monk, still seemingly in a stupor, opened it. "Hello, Oscar," Bonito looking very dark and jubilant, reached for Monk's hand and then he saw Charlie sitting on the couch. "How are you, Charlie? It's good seeing you again."

"Aw, I'm okay, Bonito; it's good seeing you,

by Randolph Harris

too." Dumont lifted himself from the couch. "You guys go on with your business; I'll be in the other room."

Bonito looked at Monk as if to ask what was wrong. Needless to say, he received no aid from Monk who had problems of his own.

Agent Gruff and Miller were seated in the rear of a brown bureau car which sported Ohio license plates. Agents Phillips and Brown were seated in the front. The car was across the street from Detroit's Hilton Book Cadillac Hotel.

There was slight puzzlement among the four agents; two Black, two white. Gruff spoke. "The Chief wasted no time in contacting the Bureau here about Monk's wife. That'll cause a change of plans for him and us."

"Do you think," Brown asked, "that this guy Monk has got the news already?"

"Probably," Gruff returned, "and that leaves us wondering what will be his next move."

"It certainly fouls up everything," Miller said.

"Yeah," Brown cut in. "We could tell that the case had top priority when we were asked to fly over to one of your groupings."

A cab pulled up in front of the hotel and the agents watched in silence. Two young ladies, one blonde, the other redhead, and show types written

THE BLACK CONNECTION

all over them, got out of the cab and entered the hotel, giggling loudly.

"Well, we know Bonito is in there with Monk," Gruff said, "but I'd give my paycheck to know what they're saying."

"Whatever it is," Miller remarked, "you can bet Monk's got troubles."

"Do you think that car that brought Bonito has the stuff in it?" Phillips asked without turning his head.

"Not likely," Gruff responded. "That guy wouldn't be sitting so damned relaxed if it had." The agents were speaking of a dark blue Chevy in which a black haired man was sitting. The Chevy had brought the man and Bonito to the hotel. It was parked on the other side of the street, a little past the hotel entrance.

"Christ sakes," Gruff said, "that shipment is somewhere between here and that fucking racetrack, and we've got to grab it, not forgetting those creeps who brought it in."

"We explained to you," Agent Brown indicated, "the pattern that they followed here."

"Yeah," Phillips interjected, "but under the present conditions, no telling what kind of moves they'll make this time."

"You say we can have the use of this car?" Agent Gruff asked. "It may be that you guys will

by Randolph Harris

have to stake out Monk and his partner Dumont. What'll you do for transportation?"

"That red Pontiac up front belongs to us, too." Brown, sitting under the steering wheel, indicated the dull red coupe that was parked directly in front of the agents' car.

"How many men do we have at the racetrack, Dan?" Agent Miller seemed to be pondering.

"The Chief said that there would be eight from the Chicago branch and some from the Michigan area—that didn't include the two ladies loaned from the Detroit Police Department and those guys from Interpol. I don't know how many of them are out there waiting, but he did make it clear that two of the Interpol guys would be posing as parking attendants."

"We're pretty sure," Phillips cut in, "that the pitch last time was made at the racetrack."

"You can say that again." Agent Brown was thinking of the peculiar incidents the last time the dope dealers were in the Motor City. The agents had trailed them to the racetrack.

"What time is it?" Gruff unconsciously spoke as he gazed at his watch. "Eight-thirty." He answered his own question. "The races have started already. Come on, Monk, boy, make your move."

It was, however, another hour before Monk made a move. During that time people flowed in

THE BLACK CONNECTION

and out of the hotel. Some in groups, some with companions and of course there were many who were simply by themselves.

Cars rolled by in colorful varieties as the agents sat patiently and waited.

At 9:30, the four agents were alerted by the appearance of Monk, Charlie Dumont and Bonito Serritelli. The three men had stopped in front of the hotel entrance. Bonito Serritelli turned from the two men and briskly walked to the waiting dark blue Chevy. Monk immediately turned and followed Bonito, who by then had entered the waiting car.

There was a flexing of hands and verbal expressions by both Bonito and the man leaning from the curb with his head partially in the car window, Oscar (Monk) Davis. Dumont, on the sidewalk, was waiting.

All this was witnessed by the ever patient agents, who by now had quite furtively divided themselves into the separate cars.

It was Agents Danny Gruff and Sidney Miller who followed Bonito and his slick-haired chauffeur, leaving Agents Phillips and Brown to cover Monk and Charlie Dumont.

Agent Gruff surmised that Bonito would eventually lead them to the illicit shipment, therefore the latter became the chosen target.

by Randolph Harris

This trail led the Federal Agents through winding and crisscrossed streets.

"I'm not very familiar with this damn spider-webbed city," Gruff remarked. "Have you got your detailed diagram that the Chief issued?"

Miller reached inside his suit pocket and produced a leather folder. The Agents' car was taking them past tall buildings that made the streets appear as corridors. Illuminated lights from turning beams reflected against huge monsters with glowing electric eyes. All of which brought them to a gigantic school of slow moving cars.

"I think we're right on target for the Windsor Racetrack. According to this diagram," said Miller, whose pock-marked features showed from the glare of the dashboard light. "This," Miller indicated, "should be the late racetrack traffic. The border should be at the other end of this shuttle."

"I hope that damn shipment is at the other end," Gruff answered.

Arriving in Canada, the land of Her Majesty, the Federal Agents kept the dark blue car in constant view as the bevy of traffic spilled into the parking area of Windsor Racetrack, the home of Canada's night trotting races.

Charlie Dumont and Oscar (Monk) Davis, unaware that two Federal Agents were dogmatically

THE BLACK CONNECTION

stalking their every movement, hailed a cab and instructed the driver to Detroit's Metropolitan Airport. And very shortly, they boarded the plane.

Agent Roscoe E. Brown made his way to a convenient telephone booth. Federal Agents of the Chicago Division would be awaiting the plane's arrival, where they would take up the dope dealers' trail.

Charlie Dumont was very silent, as was his companion, Monk. Unlike their last returning plane trip, Monk gazed out into the blanket of ebony and it at once reminded him of his foreseeable future—black, ominous and indeed quite dubious. It really seemed inconceivable that what had taken him years to build could so abruptly be completely destroyed. Every one of his loyal subordinates had met with violent ends, and last, but not least, the most faithful one of all was now gone. Sonya, yes, Sonya, whom he would always turn to when things looked bleak. It appeared to Monk that someone had outlined a most ingenious plan with its total function designed for his outright destruction.

In retrospect, Monk stubbornly conceded that only fate could have brought about the gatherings of such forces, and this only added to his presently frustrated dilemma. Where could he get another bankroll and start all over again? From these unpredictable occurrences he now had lost his

by Randolph Harris

connection and realized with the utmost sincerity that he could easily have lost his life.

Don Serritelli will be furious risking Bonito's safety and that of his underlings and, of course, it would be rather compelling when heaped atop fantastic expenditures that included the unexpected return of the prohibited drugs.

Oscar (Monk) Davis secretly glanced at his travelling companion who was also his childhood friend, or was he? Even he, Charlie, of late, had acted quite strangely. Was there no end to this road of despondency?

An attractive brunette stewardess, who really should have been travelling the airways to stardom, interrupted Monk's thoughts with the suggestions of coffee or tea. Both Monk and Charlie refused.

It was profoundly strange that Charlie Dumont hadn't uttered a word during the entire flight.

Unknown to the peddlers of misery, two men were following them when they deplaned. Agents Ronald Monihan ahd Jeffrey Boyd, due to the shortage of men who had presently been assigned duty at the racetrack in Canada, were instructed by the Chicago Field Office to disband surveillance of Monk's apparently empty house, then proceed to O'Hare Airport and keep the two suspects, Oscar (Monk) Davis and Charlie Dumont under close surveillance. Pending the outcome of the operation

THE BLACK CONNECTION

in Canada, a Federal warrant for their arrest on charges of conspiracy to buy, sell and distribute narcotics was being prepared.

Monk and Dumont hailed a cab and left the airport. Traffic along the Dan Ryan Expressway has a tendency to thin after midnight, and so it was as the cab took Monk and Dumont along Chicago's busiest thoroughfare. They eventually left the Dan Ryan and finally poured onto Lake Shore Drive, the city's beautiful scenic shore line. The cabbie steered into Yates Boulevard and continued south. Monk, nervous and clearly apprehensive, was sitting sideways in the rear of the cab. He was talking to Dumont.

"I'll go by the house and get some clothes, then go over to Dolly's apartment."

Dumont gave Monk a casual nod and appeared to be thinking.

The neighborhood appeared peaceful and quiet, no traffic at this hour. But wait, Monk focused through the rear window. "Driver," Monk exclaimed, without changing his stare, "turn at the next corner."

The driver obeyed and turned the wheel. Monk, still gazing past the rear window, saw the pair of headlights turn also. Monk felt that it couldn't possibly be the green station wagon. Dolly had already explained the car and Sonya when he'd

by Randolph Harris

made the telephone call in Detroit. Maybe it was some of the Black Angels seeking further revenge?

"Turn right again, driver." Monk never turned his head from the window.

"What is it, man?" Charlie finally asked, glancing back.

"Those lights, they're following us!" It was hard for anyone to determine what kind of a car it was. As Monk had truthfully stated, all he could see were those two headlights.

In the confusion of turning, the cab was now on South Chicago Avenue, heading east.

Monk, perspiring heavily, shouted again. "Turn here, man!" Obediently, the driver steered the cab right onto Cottage Grove and speeded up a bit. Again the trailing headlights turned. However, the well-lit avenue enabled Monk to visualize the mysterious trailing car along with its two occupants. It was a dark brown car, but the two passengers were quite indistinguishable.

"Quick! Turn right here," Monk almost screamed. "Now wait here a minute. I'll be right back!"

The cab was on the 64th Street side of the Pershing Hotel. The confused cab driver looked back at the relaxed Charlie Dumont and obeyed Monk's command.

"Be right back, Charlie," Monk repeated as he

THE BLACK CONNECTION

dashed from the cab. It wasn't closing time as Monk entered the Pershing lounge bar. A few hangers-on topped leather-capped stools as Monk sauntered through. He quickened his steps as he went through the alcove that led into the lobby. Monk, furtively, though most quickly, made his way into the livery cab office which was directly off the lobby entrance. There he chose one of the livery drivers and left from the Cottage Grove entrance of the hotel. The cabbie, Charlie Dumont and the agents who were parked across the street were still waiting.

Oscar (Monk) Davis instructed the livery driver to Roberts 66th Street Motel. Within the confines of the room, he simply mused. Who was in the trailing car? Who could he call? Was it safe to enter his own house? Was it safe to contact Dolly? Where would he get a bankroll? How angry would Serritelli become when Bonito returned with the unsold dope? He couldn't chance those Black Angels finding him. The chairs, dresser, television and the small writing desk never caught Monk's eye. He only lay on the bed and stared absently at the painted ceiling. He did this until sleep finally engulfed him.

To assume that Monk's slumber was quite brief would be correct, for it was when he awoke that he looked at his watch and turned on the radio. It was

by Randolph Harris

early morning. Sounds of maids closing doors, voices from people checking out, commercial trucks backing in and leaving were long forgotten happenings to Oscar (Monk) Davis. He went into the bathroom and came face to face with the mirror. Good Lord! It was frightening. Maybe he should take a chance and call Dolly? At least he should have clean clothes.

Monk picked up the receiver and dialed.

Dolly, dainty, petite and looking too lovely to be alone, sat on the edge of her queen-sized bed. An ashtray half filled with cigarettes and reefer butts told a silent story. The phone rang.

"Where have you been?" Dolly inquired into the receiver. "I been calling everywhere trying to locate you. Have you seen the morning papers?" If Monk tried to answer, his effort proved nil. Dolly went on. "I guess you know they're looking for you? Why didn't you call and tell me where you were?"

Monk forced Dolly's questions to a halt. "I'll explain when I see you. What do the papers say?"

"Wait a second. It's right here on my bed." Dolly then grasped the rumpled newspaper that was already turned to page two. She reclaimed the receiver. "Here it is, listen. Forces of the Federal Narcotics Bureau, combined with squads of the Metropolitan Police and R.C.M.P. officers, armed

THE BLACK CONNECTION

with Queen's Writs, were aided by International Police in the arrest of Bonito Serritelli, Tony Spananzia and Brassi Alitori, who was killed in an attempted shootout with the arresting agents at Canada's Windsor Racetrack. Government sources said that the arrests coincided with a similar raid which netted a Haitian diplomat at a camouflaged secret airport in the Santiago Province. The source went on to say that the seizure of over two million dollars—at street value—heroin was confiscated and the arrests ended a long surveillance by all the law enforcements concerned. Federal Agents, armed with warrants, are seeking Oscar (Monk) Davis, a Black American, who is allegedly connected with the narcotics ring which was masterminded by Don Santino Serritelli, head of an eastern Mafia family." Dolly casually threw the newspaper aside. "That's what it says, word for word ... Hello? Hello, Oscar!"

Dolly could not get an answer. After making several futile efforts, she called the desk. The motel switchboard operator said that she would send the bellboy to check, that is, if Dolly would care to hold the phone. Dolly complied. After waiting a seemingly long time, she was finally told in a pleasant voice that the room was vacant and that the phone receiver was lying on the bed.

It had never been recradled.

chapter 11

IT WAS EASY TO UNDERSTAND the present confusion within the Staten Island estate of Don Santino Serritelli. Two telephones were being used and a third, within the Don's bottom desk drawer, was ringing.

Consigliori Mario Fanazi, standing at the corner of the desk and facing the Don, was busily speaking Sicilian lingo into one phone. The other was being used by the Don himself.

Sadness and ill-luck had cast dark shadows over the Family Serritellis. Bonito and Tony were temporarily confined behind prison bars and a brave soldier of the Family had died on foreign soil.

THE BLACK CONNECTION

Eloquently phrased messages were received throughout the day. Even the troublesome Galanos, who figured that deaths such as Brassi's should only happen amongst their own, had showed brotherhood and sent words of kind thought.

Fanazi had completed his call. He cradled the phone receiver and stood gazing past the window out onto the spacious, manicured lawns. The Dobermans were frolicking playfully, though their appearances left no doubt that, need be, their folly would become spontaneously virulent.

Don Serritelli had ended his phone conversation and, twisting his tall, black leather swivel chair, spoke quite casually. "It is I who is to blame for these terrible mishaps. Had I listened to you, my Consigliori, none of them could have occurred."

Fanazi turned and faced his Don. "Do not blame yourself, Don Serritelli. It is the Black man whom I fault. From our Chicago friends, it is rumored that no one has seen or heard from him. I fear he, as a Black man, does not know the code of the *omerta*. If he has not talked already, when subdued, he no doubt will."

Don Serritelli reached to the bottom drawer of the desk and lifted his private phone. "I would have no need of you were I to ignore your advice. I'll make sure that we have nothing to fear from

by Randolph Harris

this Black man."

A phone rang in a dingy Brooklyn apartment as two young Italians sat across from each other playing cards. The table would surely have made any antique dealer rejoiceful.

The smell of spaghetti and garlic scented the unsightly, ill-kept apartment. Angrily, the tallest of the two unshaven men slammed down the cards and lifted the phone. "Si." The man spoke no other words and momentarily he hung up. And so instead of returning to his card game, he strolled to the clothes closet and from the pocket of a seldom used jacket, he removed a handful of shotgun shells.

Much later that night, this same man was seen boarding a Chicago bound plane. His appearance, however, had undergone an amazing change. He was donned in an expensively tailored blue suit and highly polished leather shoes. His custom-made white shirt was accented by an imported cravat. To the average focus, his true profession was amiss. How could anyone clearly distinguish that he was a professional assassin?

Back in Chicago, Agents Gruff and Miller were leaving the post office. They had just left the office of Robert E. Bennett, United States Marshal, and had had a briefing on their latest narcotics raid about which Marshal Bennett had made certain points quite specific.

"You know, Sid, the marshal was right," Gruff indicated as they approached the parking lot. "We were expecting to nail Monk and Dumont at that racetrack along with Bonito and those other creeps, but we couldn't predict the death of his wife and the other things. With his affluent way of living and other evidence we've accumulated, Monk could be tied in rather easily. But like the marshal said, even though we know that guy Dumont is involved, we'll have a tough time presenting evidence to that effect. Of course, Mr. Monk has got his lumps already. You know, the I.R.S. salvaged the majority of that burnt money, and now they're looking for him, too."

"That's justice," Miller uttered as he opened the door of the green sedan bearing the Tennessee license plates. The October day was brisk and sunny as the agents rode along Lake Street going east. They appeared mindless of the humdrum traffic that continued to cross them. Michigan Avenue was exceedingly busy. The agents' green car rounded the Prudential Building, cruised out on Randolph Street and turned south at Lake Shore Drive. The scenic boats and yachts had disappeared from Lake Michigan in expectation of the coming winter. Buckingham Fountain had ceased its mag-

by Randolph Harris

nificent flow and trees along the shore had accepted a mild hue of brown.

The green car was passing gigantic Soldier's Field when Miller spoke. "I don't know if we'll reach the guy in time, since the word's around that the Family's put out a contract on him."

"Yeah," Gruff said, displaying some of his hidden compassion. "The poor devil doesn't realize he'd be better off giving up to us."

The green car continued south.

Charlie Dumont had just returned from the hospital. The doctor had told him that his mother, Mrs. Dumont, had suffered a mild stroke. She would have to be confined, but with proper mental and physical care would probably recover.

Charlie passed through his mother's bedroom. Jimmy's room was off to the side. The apartment, to Charlie, suddenly became a void. He noticed a newspaper lying on his mother's bed. It was turned to page two. Dumont thought to himself. He had told his mother that Monk was the man he worked for in the wide-spread numbers game.

Charlie held back the swelling within himself. He had an urge to explode with the remorse that had engulfed his entire being. He, himself, by all moral and conscientious convictions, had destroyed those who made up his entire world. Turbulently, he

THE BLACK CONNECTION

strolled to his room, and from under his bed he removed a long cardboard box. It was a few moments later when Dumont was sitting at the kitchen table. He was eyeing the Xeroxed pages as he turned them. They appeared to be a novel, a manuscript, or perhaps just some books.

Quite meticulously, Charlie used the razor blade as he went about cutting portions of print from various pages. He piled these small pieces in an ashtray and set them on fire. It shouldn't have astounded anyone that all these pieces bore the name Charlie Dumont. As he deleted his name from the pages, Charlie thought about Monk. Monk hadn't even called to explain about leaving him sitting there in the cab. Humph! thought Charlie. Monk and that bullshit about someone following! Oh, well, even if that were true, what fucking difference would it make now?

Completing the task of his deletions, Charlie addressed the package and left the apartment. He stopped on 63rd at Cottage Grove Avenue, parked his car and walked to the mail box. He dropped the package. And so, after returning to his car and driving away, he reached and lit a cigarette, then thought, "It was just something that had to be done."

It was on Chicago's indigent west side. Monk,

by Randolph Harris

tall, slunking and bearing that all too familiar look of a hunted man, peered into the mirror that was on the wall of the stagnant toilet. The entire block of structural eyesores was long past the schedule for condemning. This room in which Monk had lived for the last few days was part of the B. and F. Hotel, a red brick building that boasted six floors and an elevator which often times did not operate.

Monk feebly stroked his face as he stared at the stubble. How pronounced fate had become with its dogmatic intentions to destroy him. Incidents of the past few days would have disintegrated lesser men. Perhaps that long indoctrination of survival endured within the ghetto had brought him thus far. It was becoming, however, most apparent that those ideological substances were ebbing by degrees.

Monk stepped from the cubicle that served as a bathroom. He entered another enclosure that was slightly larger. Boards swollen, humped and loose caused the floor to be uneven. Freshly plastered holes did the dirty walls a further injustice. The bed held a mattress that was rounded on the edges like an obese woman's hangings, and the window panes with tape proved the glass had been injured. Monk stared out from one of these. He was watching for Dolly. He had held out as long as possible. She had sounded happy to hear from him, but that remained to be seen.

Monk thought of Dumont. But it was a sure thing the agents would be watching Charlie. Monk, however, presumed that the agents were unaware of Dolly. If she was careful and watched herself, she could make it without being trailed, even if the agents did know about her. Anyway, damn it, he had no alternative.

It was after five o'clock in the evening. Monk could tell by the people who were getting off buses and the heavy traffic on Pulaski Boulevard. Runny-nosed children dashed in and out of candy shops, some buying and some learning the rip-off at an early age. A group of teenage boys were gathered outside Mike's Poolhall. Mike, himself, was across the street in the rear of Bob's Chicken Shack. They played craps back there.

Six floors up, Monk stood behind the cracked and dirty hotel window, watching. And shortly, a northbound bus came to a stop at the corner. Monk had patiently instructed Dolly to board the El train and then transfer to a bus. There she was—obedient girl—stepping from a crowded bus of workers. Dolly did a feminine trot across the boulevard, then she paused beneath the dingy white bulb of a street light. The low glowing bulb displayed the letters "Hot"; the last two letters were missing. Quickly, she darted through the

by Randolph Harris

deteriorating entrance and made her way to the elevator. This time, it did operate. Entering the elevator, Dolly, small, brown and lovely, began the squeaking journey to the sixth floor.

How was she to know that Agents Gruff and Miller had traced her every move? She and Gruff had boarded the El train at almost the same time, only he had entered the other end of the same coach car. With the aid of his pocket-sized talkie, Miller was waiting to pick him up when Dolly had transfered to the evening bus. The rest was quite simple.

As has happened with the hunter and the hunted, so it was that the trailer became the trailed.

But, of course, what better method for an assassin to find his prey than to follow others who were also seeking the same. The agents' car continued to cruise while Dolly went through the hotel entrance.

"Turn this corner and park," Gruff said. "I'll go see what the set-up is. He's in there somewhere."

Farther back, the stranger from New York ceased his sleuthing of the agents' car. He now was tailing Dolly as his agile legs sprinted him across the busy boulevard. When the young Italian spotted Agent Gruff approaching the hotel entrance, he continued past. The assassin carried an

THE BLACK CONNECTION

innocent looking attache case as he strolled.

It was moments later when Gruff returned to the green Bureau car. He sat in the front seat next to his partner.

"Like I said, Monk's in that fire trap somewhere, but it's a real soul den. A white face show up in there and the whole place would start buzzing."

"Okay, so what's our next move?" Miller looked at his partner, waiting.

"Well, first of all," Gruff was scanning the terrain as he talked, "call the Chief and ask him to put a cover around the hotel. I'm going back and find out what room Monk's holed up in." Gruff's hand was on the door lever.

"Be careful, Danny. The guy knows everybody is trying to take him out. He'll be dangerous."

"Yeah, I know. After you talk to the Chief, keep that front entrance covered, I'm going to try it from the back."

"Gotcha," Miller answered while reaching for the dashboard telephone.

Darkness had blanketed the decayed locale as Dolly sat on the edge of Monk's bed. "I brought you the paper so you could read about yourself. Why did you do it, Oscar? Didn't you realize they'd find you someday?"

Dolly looked neat and petite. Monk's shadow resembled that of a bush.

by Randolph Harris

"I wish I could truthfully blame everything on myself. It was just a bad chain of events." Monk was busy opening packages. He continued, "Those large purses come in handy, don't they?" Monk eyed Dolly's large leather bag.

"Well, you told me to be extra careful. I certainly didn't want to show any packages. When are you going to leave this place?"

Dolly looked about with disgust. Monk bit down on the cold corned beef sandwich and answered between bites, "I'm hoping to leave the city tonight. Morris is bringing me some bread from Gary. Look, Dolly, I want you to get in touch with Charlie, nobody else. Just him, you understand?"

Dolly raised her knees and crossed them sideways. She was leaning on her elbow. Monk was on the other side of the bed.

"Yeah," Dolly answered, looking up. "I'll find Charlie. The word's out that he's not seen around anymore. Are you and him still tight?"

"Yeah. We're all right." Monk swallowed the warm pop, then spoke again. "Charlie went through a thing when his kid brother O.D.'d but that was no more than natural. Charlie, I mean."

"You know, I wish you the best, Monk, but," Dolly looked up through heavily made-up eyes, "they've gotcha up tight, man. And if you don't quit the scene, somebody's gonna take you out."

THE BLACK CONNECTION

Dolly thought she heard a tinge of contrition as Monk reached for a rusty tin ashtray. "Aw, I'll be okay once Morris gets here. But, you know what, baby? I still can't see how everything happened so fast. Maybe I got conned somewhere along the way. I thought I had everything figured. I intended to beat the system and forget it." A plane droned overhead and it shook the building.

Dolly straightened from her leaning position. "You know, I dig you, big fellow, but you can't expect me to go for this." Dolly flicked her hands and looked directly at Monk.

"No, baby," Monk leaned back his head and blew smoke above his stubby chin, "I always knew where we were at. I dug you, and I'd like to think that you dug me. I had some bread and you were needing." Monk moved over to the dirty cracked windows and looked out.

"Don't make it sound so damn cold, Oscar. Sure I was needing, but, damn it, I was needing a man, too. Many a night I've tossed and turned thinking about you and Sonya. I'm not going to say that I'm sorry she was taken out. I'd be a lying bitch if I did. Oh, I know, she was your wife and all that. But I want you to know that I did dig you and I still do. But you've got a tough road ahead, Monk. And I just don't think I can cut it." Dolly eyed the .45 automatic in Monk's belt.

by Randolph Harris

"I dig, baby. You just slow me down anyhow." Monk was answering while he peered through the window. The old elevator was clanking its way up and down the decaying shaft.

Outside, in the rear, the New Yorker had made his way to the higher roof of the building next door. He leaped and landed about six feet below with his attache case in his hand. He now was atop the B.F. Hotel. Cautiously he stepped around the huge TV antenna. His crepe-soled shoes made mild crunching sounds as he stealthily crept along the tar red and pebbled roof. The New Yorker's dark blue suit blended with the fast appearing night as he ambulated in guerilla fashion. He peered over the front of the decrepit hotel.

Pulaski Boulevard was still active. Cabs, buses and cars were in abundance as people flowed up, down and across the busy thoroughfare. Assorted hues from the many neon signs made his downward glance quite pleasing. To the sinister stranger, things indeed appeared to be in the norm. He glanced about the roof. His gaze outlined a wooden structure. Its ceiling appeared to be slanted downward into the hotel roof. On further investigation, the ominous stranger found the structure had a wooden door.

He entered and discovered some downward stairs. Fixtures operating the elevator were en-

THE BLACK CONNECTION

closed by heavy steel wire mesh. Giant, greasy black wheels turned forward and then backward as old linked chains squeaked, clanked and slowly lifted the ancient cubicle. A much used door, also made of steel wire mesh, was slightly ajar. The stranger noticed it.

It was for the availability of repairmen who made repeated trips of aid to the decaying mass of machinery. The Italian youth used gloved hands to open the wire mesh door. He leaned inside and peered down. He saw the top of the elevator float to the sixth floor and stop. Its ceiling was directly in front of him. In fact, he could have stepped on the elevator roof as it floated down again. He pushed the wire gate shut and began to sleuth out his prey. His gloved hand gripped the attache case tightly.

chapter 12

MEANWHILE, AGENT DANNY GRUFF, using the fire escape, had gained entrance to the hotel through a side window on the second floor. He had mounted the rear stairs of the building next door when he spotted the slightly raised window. The narcotics agent found himself in a rather dirty plastered hallway. Doors were standing ajar while some were locked with varying sounds floating out. The hallway appeared L-shaped and there was a mixture of voices approaching from the far end. Gruff hastily glanced about, no place to hide and less time to do it. The voices were almost upon him.

Immediately Gruff went into a slumping position; his hat brim bent forward—a mild attempt to hide his face. His coat and pants pocket linings were hanging out as he leaned facing the grimy wall, drunkenly humming and reciting, "Mary had a little lamb."

THE BLACK CONNECTION

Three persons, two ladies and a male, all wearing Afros, cast a few giggling remarks and passed him by. It was not until he'd reached the bend of the L-shaped hall and had the assurance of the fading voices that he straightened and went about his clandestine research.

Dolly had taken the creeping elevator down and Monk had seated himself on the bed, awaiting Morris. He unfolded the paper. The headlines confronted him! "Fugitive's Personal Books Received by U.S. Marshal, Anonymously."

Monk straightened; how did it happen? His mind became computerized. The books that Charlie had returned were well concealed. Sonya was dead. How? Whatever the answer, Charlie Dumont had to be at fault. Charlie! Dolly was going to tell him where Monk was hiding out. So that was what Dolly meant when she'd asked Monk why they'd done it? Dolly had read the paper and thought he, Monk, had mailed the books. Monk had to stop her. But he couldn't leave. Morris was bringing him some money. But he had to stop Dolly.

Monk sprang from the bed and in a step had reached the door. He bounded down the hall to the old elevator. Through the open wire mesh he could see the top of the elevator going down. He couldn't wait. He had to overtake Dolly. Oscar dashed to the creaking stairs and scrambled down. He heard

by Randolph Harris

the door of the elevator cage clank open, then the door slide back. He had reached the third floor. His breath was coming extremely fast. Monk started down; he heard the elevator coming up. He waited. Ah, it had passed the second floor. It was coming to the third floor level. Oh, no! It kept going up! Monk started his desperate scramble down the stairs again.

He was nearing the so-called lobby; a small cage with slots for keys and mail was in the background. No one was on duty. An old flower pot held a dying plant and next to a wooden bench sat a lop-sided cigarette machine. It took more money without providing returns than a fixed slot machine.

Monk approached the main floor in a huff. He was still breathing fast and excitedly as he rushed thought the door leading to the sidewalk. He looked up and down the street. It was then that he saw the white man with the pock-marked face spring from the green sedan across the street.

Oscar (Monk) Davis reached to his belt and grasped the heavy .45. He started to run toward the corner but he saw two white men coming directly at him. They were reaching inside their coats.

Monk fired at the two men and at the same time heard a loud command from across the street.

THE BLACK CONNECTION

"Drop that gun. Federal Agents!"

Monk turned, intending to shoot in the direction of the voice, but heard another loud explosion and instantly felt a jolt that knocked him back into the hotel door. Monk fired another shot as two or three pellets made zinging sounds from bullets grazing the building. He pushed backward against the hotel door. It yielded and he was back in the small, smelly lobby. He had been hit in the shoulder. Blood was drenching him as he fired two more shots in the direction of the door.

Confusion had taken hold of the hotel's occupants. Doors were opened and slammed. Voices from the above floors were yelling out in wonderment.

The elevator reached the lobby level with a thud and its cage door clanged open. Then the elevator door slid back. No one was in it. Monk, wounded, bleeding and desperate, looked at the open elevator as a Godsend. He dashed from his crouched position behind the clerk's cage and practically fell into the waiting elevator. Monk fired a shot through the wire-mesh as the elevator carried his wounded body up. He had pressed the sixth floor button. Perhaps he could escape over the rooftops. Damn, the elevator was too fucking slow. It had only reached the third floor.

Monk's mind was trying to supply the multitude

by Randolph Harris

of answers. Where did all the whiteys come from? Maybe they were Federal Agents and maybe not. He recalled times when stick-up and hit men had used the ruse successfully. Besides, what difference did it make? They were all out to get him. The elevator, it was coming to the sixth floor level. Then suddenly the escape hatch of the elevator sprang open. With surprise on his face, Monk looked up. The last thing Oscar (Monk) Davis saw on this earth were two holes at the end of a double-barreled shotgun. The blasts were heard throughout the area.

Agent Gruff, at the time, was on the fifth floor in one of the L-shaped hallways. He had been listening.

Agent Miller, after exchanging shots and wounding Monk, accompanied the covering agents and had entered the hotel in pursuit of their prey. Miller bounded up the steps. He was yelling with his pistol in his hand. "Danny! Danny! Are you all right?"

Miller was on the second floor enroute to the third when he heard his partner's voice. "Up here, Sid, I'm on the sixth floor. Cover this elevator, I'm going to the roof. I'm damn sure the killer's up there!"

Gruff took a parting look at the remains of Monk's body. Crimson splattered the elevator enclosure and then made downward trails. Gruff hurriedly placed his white handkerchief over the stub that once had been a neck. As he departed, the white material, like everything else inside the elevator, had turned blood red.

The curious entered the hallways and filtered from within the shoddy rooms. Gruff yelled to Miller who was taking the stairs two at a time. "Don't let anyone move this elevator. See that that 'stop' button stays on!"

Agent Gruff was going up the stairs. He passed the repairmen's wire mesh gate and proceeded to the wooden steps; these led to the roof. Gruff noticed the pronounced dampness of his hand as he regripped his pistol. Through the years he'd often times played out this same scene, and it was always comparable to the first; the same apprehensiveness, the same excitement and above all the same unrelenting dedication.

Gruff knew the killer was still on the roof. There had been no reports over his talkie from the area's cover men. He cautiously opened the weather-beaten door that spilled onto the roof. Slowly, quite slowly, he widened the door. Cover agents who had followed Agent Miller were now coming up the steps to the aid of Agent Gruff.

Gruff, squatting in the open door, cautioned them to stay down. He viewed the roof's terrain

by Randolph Harris

and spotted curved air-ducts, an air-conditioning unit that appeared out of order, and a skylight that was built like a miniature house. He looked back at the two agents who were crouched on the stairs.

"I'll make it to that skylight," Gruff said. "You guys take it from there. He's up here someplace. He'll have to make his pitch damn soon."

The cool October night was bright and clear. Gruff made his dash and there came a loud explosion. Gruff reached the skylight. Glass and debris flew into the night as half of the skylight disintegrated. The young assassin had exposed his location with the flash from his deadly shotgun. The covering agents from within the stairs concentrated their shots on that particular spot. Needless to say, the agile young Italian had moved. Then another loud explosion dominated the night, and this one removed the other half of the shattered skylight. The two cover agents felt quite relieved when they learned that Agent Gruff had already changed his position.

"We're Federal Agents," Gruff yelled out. We're asking you to drop your gun and surrender!"

Agent Gruff quickly moved from the spot and crouched behind a large air duct. He did right. A blast from the shotgun completely removed what looked to be a small chimney. It was, however, to be the Italian's last voluntary act.

THE BLACK CONNECTION

The covering agents were patiently awaiting that shotgun flash. The young assassin never had a chance to duck down. He was propelled backward through the air by the force from the agents' shots.

It was the following morning. Slick, the bartender at the 808 Club, was cleaning the bar of dirty glasses. He noticed the morning paper had been left by his only customer. Slick glanced at the headlines and his motions at work became lax. It was simple. "Books of Slain Narcotics Dealer Reveals All."

The paper went on to give names of Alderman James (Big Jim) Sanders, Police Captain LaVerne Peterson, Commander of Chicago's gigantic Fifth District, and Detective First Class John Poindexter. The paper went on to give other astounding information concerning the dope operation on Chicago's south side. It was made quite clear to all that the intricate dope operation could not have existed without the sanctioning of those higher up in authority.

The government promised that there would be indictments handed down.

City Hall made a show of being completely surprised. His Honor, the Mayor, held a press conference and stated that it was outsiders who had brought these terrible drugs to the fine commu-

by Randolph Harris

nities of Chicago.

A few days later, Agents Danny Gruff and his partner Sidney Miller were on the Calumet Expressway. They were on their way to Gary, Indiana.

"Well, Sid," Gruff said, "I hope this operation isn't as nerve-wracking as the last."

"You know, Danny, I think you're right about those books. The only one who could have possibly sent them was Charlie Dumont. I think the death of his kid brother turned him around."

"Yeah, that was some helluva pressure for the guy, especially after his mother had that stroke."

"By the way, Danny, did you ever get word on what happened to Dumont?"

"Naw, Sid, it seems he just up and disappeared."

It was six months later, in St. Louis, Missouri at the Beckman Rehabilitation Center, a halfway house for narcotic addicts. Director Robert M. Pullens entered the office of the Assistant Administrator George B. Hawkins.

"Hi, George, I've been going over the reports, and for the last three or four months we've shown an amazing increase in potential cures."

George Hawkins, Black, horn-rimmed glasses, and hair steel-grey at the temples, removed his glasses and wiped them.

THE BLACK CONNECTION

"I was wondering when you would take notice. It all adds up to one of my new assistants. He walked in here one day and said that he wanted a job, any thing or any kind, just so long as he could help." Hawkins replaced his glasses. "And you know what? The fellow seems to have a certain understanding with the boys, especially the younger ones. He devotes all his time. He's forever holding classes. I have actually never seen a person more dedicated. I've often tried to talk to him, to draw him out about his past, but he always avoids the subject, so," Hawkins gestured with his hands, "I don't rock the boat."

"Well, the first chance you think is right," the Director pointed out, "I'd like to have a few words with him." As he started out the door, Pullens turned and asked, "By the way, what is that fellow's name?"

"Oh, it's Charlie Dumont."

Afterword

It is a widely known fact that truth and reality have often been the objects of concealment and denial; from the era of the Teapot Dome to the present day Watergate affair. The book you now hold, I suspect, will receive similar treatment from some special groups. But, deny if they can that what you read here is true. The records will surely bear this out.

Resonant voices from Black brothers and sisters will decry the violence and degradation as though that alone is the purpose of this endeavor. Yell as they might, can they disclaim that eighty percent of illegal hard drugs are bought, sold, and distributed in the Black community? They can't. Some

THE BLACK CONNECTION

may deplore the subject with the most sincere honesty. That alone gives reason number one for this book's being.

To enlighten persons of the destitute and violent surroundings in which they live, is not always accepted with amiability. That, however, does not mean that these existences should not be stressed.

If unawareness is the case, and they, the deplorers, are candid in their denunciations, it gives all the more for reason number two for this book. If this gathering of words is sustained by young or old, they not only tend to create knowledge of the plight and chaos that is caused by the use and distribution of these terrible drugs. They also tend to show that because those in authority ignored its existence for so long as it was in the Black locale, they failed to foresee the inevitable overspill that would eventually bring about the same plight and chaos to this affluent country in its entirety. This has become a blatant fact of life in America today.

You can be safe in assuming that this only could have been written by one who knows thoroughly the workings within the Ghetto and the psychological motivations which prompted the ghetto's inhabitants—mainly escape.

Is escapism an excuse? No. But rather, an ostensible fact. The ghetto being an obviously fertile dump for the higher echelons of destruction even-

by Randolph Harris

ually brought on contacts and connections. What better reasons, I ask you, than to call this book THE BLACK CONNECTION?

This book is fictional, but if you've ever lived in Chicago, you'll know it's true.

R.H.

THE TERRORISTS

By Randolph Harris

Who were the very clever people hitting top secret government installations and stealing vital secrets—and materials with such ease? They certainly weren't the old style liberal radicals. And they didn't seem to be agents of foreign government and they *were* connected to Professor Brock, the brilliant and very wealthy black scientist who had supposedly defected to Russia after his son was killed during a college demonstration for peace. It soon became clear that Brock was not in Russia, but was using his vast resources to build a nuclear bomb and had recruited top-of-the-line college students and not raving radicals—to his very dangerous organization!

Somewhere out there a man planned to blow up the world!

HOLLOWAY HOUSE PUBLISHING CO.
8060 MELROSE AVE., LOS ANGELES, CA 90046

Gentlemen: I enclose $_____ ☐ cash, ☐ check, ☐ money order, payment in full for books ordered. I understand that if I am not completely satisfied, I may return my order within 10 days for a complete refund. (Add 75 cents per order to cover postage. California residents add 6½% sales tax. Please allow three weeks for delivery.)

☐ **BH283-5 THE TERRORISTS $2.50**

Name _____

Address _____

City _____ State _____ Zip _____

SCARS AND MEMORIES: THE STORY OF A LIFE

By Odie Hawkins

Scars and Memories is Odie Hawkins' deeply personal story of his life's journey, from a childhood in Chicago where he was one of the "poorest of the poor" to highly paid Hollywood screenwriter with his own office—and those people, mostly women, who mattered to him along the way. *Scars and Memories* is a tough, gritty book about a survivor who, as a child, lived in dank, cold tenement basements where the cockroaches were so thick on the walls he could set fire to them with rolled up newpapers, where there was seldom enough food, where sex and drugs were as commonplace as summer rain and winter chill. This is a deeply personal story, sometimes painfully told, that only a writer of Hawkins maturity and skill could write. Odie Hawkins is the author of the novels *Chicago Hustle, Chili, The Busting Out of An Orindary Man, Ghetto Sketches* and *Sweet Peter Deeder*

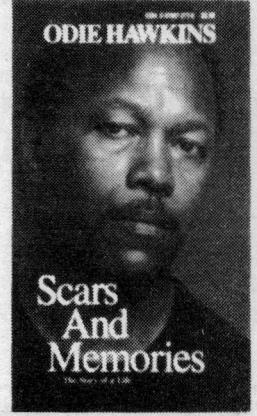

HOLLOWAY HOUSE PUBLISHING CO.
8060 MELROSE AVE., LOS ANGELES, CA 90046

Gentlemen: I enclose $_____ ☐ cash, ☐ check, ☐ money order, payment in full for books ordered. I understand that if I am not completely satisfied, I may return my order within 10 days for a complete refund. (Add 75 cents per order to cover postage. California residents add 6½% sales tax. Please allow three weeks for delivery.) ☐ **BH277-0 SCARS AND MEMORIES, $2.50**

Name _____

Address _____

City _____ State _____ Zip _____

STREET WARS
By Joe Nazel

There was a bunch of creeps selling dope to Los Angeles kids from ice cream trucks and Our Man Slaughter, a former cop turned detective, is out to get them. It appears for a while that he's taken on a war that not even an enemy could win as his chase (and what a chase it is!) takes him from the sewers to the sacred and traditional power base of the black community— the churches! To complicate matters, there is one gang selling dope to the kids of another, a group of fanatical black militants left over from the Sixties who are trying to steal the gang's money to start a revolution— and they all are after a pretty schoolteacher who may or may not know where a bunch of money is stashed! The author of *Uprising, Killer Cop, Delta Crossing*, etc., has come up with a real page turner!

HOLLOWAY HOUSE PUBLISHING CO.
8060 MELROSE AVE., LOS ANGELES, CA 90046

Gentlemen: I enclose $_____ ☐ cash, ☐ check, ☐ money order, payment in full for books ordered. I understand that if I am not completely satisfied, I may return my order within 10 days for a complete refund. (Add 75 cents per order to cover postage. California residents add 6½% sales tax. Please allow three weeks for delivery.)

☐ **BH284-3 STREET WARS $2.50**

Name _____

Address _____

City _____ State _____ Zip _____

BLACK RENEGADES

By James Howard Readus

Fiction: Charles and Robert Jackson—C.J. and R.J.—were one ruthless pair. They had to be, as building their own dope-dealing empire meant dealing with many enemies: the pigs in their black-and-whites, the big syndicate pushers who always controlled the city's traffic . . . even their own runners who tried to increase their share of the take. The result could only be violence, and a string of shattered corpses that constantly grew longer. For a while, they relied on clever lawyers to get them off. But that took care of only one enemy: the law. The others were always there, always growing stronger and more revengeful. Until finally C.J. and R.J. stood virtually alone against a world that was—to a great extent—of their making . . . they became THE BLACK RENEGADES!

HOLLOWAY HOUSE PUBLISHING CO.
8060 MELROSE AVE., LOS ANGELES, CA 90046

Gentlemen: I enclose $_____ ☐ cash, ☐ check, ☐ money order, payment in full for books ordered. I understand that if I am not completely satisfied, I may return my order within 10 days for a complete refund. (Add 75 cents per order to cover postage. California residents add 6½% sales tax. Please allow three weeks for delivery.)   ☐ **BH294-0, BLACK RENEGADES, $2.50**

Name _____

Address _____

City _____ State _____ Zip _____

THE BLACK EXPERIENCE FROM HOLLOWAY HOUSE

★ ICEBERG SLIM

AIRTIGHT WILLE & ME (BH269-X)	$2.50
NAKED SOUL OF ICEBERG SLIM (BH713-6)	2.95
PIMP: THE STORY OF MY LIFE (BH850-7)	3.25
LONG WHITE CON (BH030-1)	2.25
DEATH WISH (BH824-8)	2.95
TRICK BABY (BH827-2)	3.25
MAMA BLACK WIDOW (BH828-0)	3.25

★ DONALD GOINES

BLACK GIRL LOST (BH042-5)	$2.25
DADDY COOL (BH041-7)	2.25
ELDORADO RED (BH067-0)	2.25
STREET PLAYERS (BH034-4)	2.25
INNER CITY HOODLUM (BH033-6)	2.25
BLACK GANGSTER (BH263-0)	2.45
CRIME PARTNERS (BH029-8)	2.25
SWAMP MAN (BH026-3)	2.25
NEVER DIE ALONE (BH018-2)	2.25
WHITE MAN'S JUSTICE BLACK MAN'S GRIEF (BH027-1)	2.25
KENYATTA'S LAST HIT (BH024-7)	2.25
KENYATTA'S ESCAPE (BH071-9)	2.25
CRY REVENGE (BH069-7)	2.25
DEATH LIST (BH070-0)	2.25
WHORESON (BH046-8)	2.25
DOPEFIEND (BH044-1)	2.25
DONALD WRITES NO MORE (BH017-4)	2.25

(A Biography of Donald Goines by Eddie Stone)

**AVAILABLE AT ALL BOOKSTORES OR ORDER FROM:
HOLLOWAY HOUSE, P.O. BOX 69804, LOS ANGELES, CA 90069
(NOTE: ENCLOSED 50¢ PER BOOK TO COVER POSTAGE.
CALIFORNIA RESIDENTS ADD 6% SALES TAX.)**